The Gingerbread Girls

Coming together in time for Christmas

The Gingerbread Inn is where best friends Emily, Andrea and Casey spent much of their childhood. Now all grown-up, they're back—older, wiser, but still with as much need of a little Massachusetts magic as ever. As Christmas approaches, and three gorgeous men appear on the scene, is it time to create some new treasured memories?

Don't miss

HER SECRET LITTLE BABY BUMP
by Shirley Jump in October 2013

MARRY ME UNDER THE MISTLETOE
by Rebecca Winters in November 2013

And SNOWFLAKES AND SILVER LININGS
by Cara Colter in December 2013

Dear Reader

You have probably heard the analogy about a duck swimming in a pond: all you see is seemingly effortless grace, a beautiful picture. But beneath the surface of the water the duck's feet are paddling like crazy!

A series like this one, about childhood friends The Gingerbread Girls, is the same way. By the time it gets to you, the reader, our hope is that all the stories fit together with effortless grace to create a beautiful total picture. But below the surface a great many people have been paddling like crazy!

Shirley took the lead on these stories and came up with a great premise and setting. Her preliminary structure made my job relatively easy. Still, you would not believe how many emails go back and forth just to name a lake! And a town. And what was the name of the dog again? And is it a male or female?

While we were working on this book, my days unfolded with, *Where is that email? What did we decide about that? Can we change that character's name? The dates of my story are making Rebecca's timeline terribly challenging. I think I made a change to my hero that I forgot to tell Shirley about....*

In the end I think the ones paddling the hardest might have been our amazing team of editors. They read carefully for inconsistencies, caught embarrassingly glaring errors and did it all with patience and grace, never losing their enthusiasm for creating the best possible story.

So my heartfelt thanks to everyone who made sure all the ducks lined up on this one!

Sincerely,

Cara Colter

Snowflakes and Silver Linings

Cara Colter

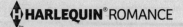

Recycling programs
for this product may
not exist in your area.

ISBN-13: 978-0-373-74271-4

SNOWFLAKES AND SILVER LININGS

First North American Publication 2013

Copyright © 2013 by Cara Colter

Printed in U.S.A.

HARLEQUIN®
www.Harlequin.com

Cara Colter lives in British Columbia with her partner, Rob, and eleven horses. She has three grown children and a grandson. She is a recipient of an *RT Book Reviews* Career Achievement Award in the Love and Laughter category. Cara loves to hear from readers, and you can contact her or learn more about her through her website, www.cara-colter.com.

Recent books by Cara Colter

HOW TO MELT A FROZEN HEART
SECOND CHANCE WITH THE REBEL*
SNOWED IN AT THE RANCH
BATTLE FOR THE SOLDIER'S HEART
THE COP, THE PUPPY AND ME
TO DANCE WITH A PRINCE
RESCUED BY HIS CHRISTMAS ANGEL
RESCUED IN A WEDDING DRESS
WINNING A GROOM IN 10 DATES

*Mothers in a Million

These and other titles by Cara Colter are available in ebook format from www.Harlequin.com

With thanks to Shirley and Rebecca

I am in awe of your creative genius, amazing discipline, and unflagging professionalism.

PROLOGUE

CHRISTMAS.

Turner Kennedy was a man who took pride in his ability not just to cope with fear, but to shape it into a different force entirely.

He had jumped from airplanes at 8,200 meters into pitch blackness and an unknown welcome.

He had raised all kinds of havoc "outside the fence" in hostile territory.

He had experienced nature's mercurial and killing moods without the benefit of shelter, sweltering heat to excruciating cold, sometimes in the same twenty-four-hour period.

He had been hungry. And lost. He had been pushed to the outer perimeters of his physical limits, and then a mile or two beyond.

He had been the hunted, stranded in the shadows of deeply inhospitable places, listening for footfalls, smelling the wind, squinting against impenetrable darkness.

It was not that he had not been afraid, but rather

that he had learned he had a rare ability to transform fear into adrenaline, power, energy.

And so the irony of his current situation was not lost on him. After a long period away, he was back in the United States, a country where safety was a given, taken for granted.

And he was afraid.

He was afraid of three things.

He was afraid of sleeping. In his dreams, he was haunted by all the things he had refused to back down from, haunted by a failure that more fear, on his part, might have changed a devastating outcome.

And maybe it was exhaustion caused by that first fear that had led to the second one.

Turner Kennedy was afraid of Christmas.

Maybe not the coming Christmas, specifically, but of his memories of ones gone by. Those memories were lingering at the edges of his mind, waiting to leap to the forefront. Today, it had been seeing an angel Christmas tree topper in a store window.

Without warning, Turner had been transported back more than two decades.

They came down the stairs, early morning light just beginning to touch the decorated living room. The tree was eight feet tall. His mother had done it all in white that year. White lights, white Christmas ornaments, a white angel on top of the tree. The house smelled of the cookies she had baked for

Santa while he and his brothers had spent Christmas Eve on the backyard skating rink their dad had made for them.

It had been past ten when his mother had finally insisted they come in. Even then, Turner hadn't wanted to. He could not get enough of the rink, of the feeling of the ice beneath his blades, of the cold on his cheeks, the wind in his hair, the power in his legs as he propelled himself forward. The whole world had seemed infused with magic....

But now the magic seemed compromised. Though the cookies were gone, nothing but crumbs remaining, Santa hadn't been there. The gifts from Santa were always left, unwrapped, right there on the hearth. This morning, that place yawned empty.

He and his younger brothers, Mitchell and David, shot each other worried looks.

Had they been bad? What had they done to fall out of Santa's favor?

His parents followed them down the steps, groggy, but seemingly unaware that anything was amiss.

"Let's open some gifts," his father said. "I've been wanting to see what's in this one."

His dad seemed so pleased with the new camera they had gone together to buy him. His mother opened perfume from Mitchell, a collectible ornament from David. She'd looked perplexed at Turn-

er's way more practical gift of a baseball mitt, and then laughed out loud.

And just as her laughter faded, Turner had heard something else.

A tiny whimper. Followed by a sharp, demanding yelp.

It was coming from the laundry room, and he bolted toward the sound before his younger brothers even heard it. In a wicker basket with a huge red bow on it was a puppy. Its fur was black and curly, its eyes such a deep shade of brown a boy could get lost in them. When Turner picked it up, it placed already huge paws on his shoulders, and leaned in, frantic with love, to lick his cheeks. Much to the chagrin of his brothers, Chaos had always loved Turner best of all....

Turner snapped himself out of it, wiped at cheeks that felt suddenly wet, as if that dog, the companion who had walked him faithfully through all the days of his childhood and teens, had licked him just now. The last time Chaos had kissed him had been over a dozen years ago, with the same unconditional love in his goodbye as had been in his hello....

To Turner's relief, his cheeks were not wet, but dry.

For the third thing he was afraid of, perhaps even more than going to sleep and the coming of Christmas, was tears.

He got up, restless, annoyed with himself.

This was the fear, exactly. That something about Christmas would weasel inside him and unleash a torrent of weakness.

He went to the barracks window. It was temporary housing, between missions. Would there be another mission? He wasn't sure if he had it in him anymore. Maybe it was time to call it quits.

But for what? It had been a long time since he had called anyplace home.

He could not stay here, at the military base, for Christmas. He hated it that emotion seemed to be breaking through his guard. It was too *empty*. There was too much room here for his own thoughts.

There was too much space for that thing he feared the most.

A yearning for the way things had once been.

David and Mitchell hadn't told him not to come for Christmas, but hadn't asked him, either. Of course, they probably assumed he was out-of-country, and he hadn't corrected that assumption.

It was better this way. He had nothing to bring to their lives. Or anyone's.

There were lots of places a single guy could go at Christmas to avoid the festivities. Palm trees had a way of dispelling that Christmassy feeling for him. A tropical resort would have the added benefit of providing all kinds of distractions. The kind of distractions that wore bikinis.

Turner was aware he wasn't getting enough

sleep. Not even the thought of women in bikinis could shake the feeling of ennui, mixed with the restless, seething energy that wouldn't let him drift off.

Just then his cell phone rang.

He must have another mission in him, after all, because he found himself hoping it was the commanding officer of his top secret Tango Force unit. That Christmas would be superseded by some world crisis.

But it wasn't his CO's number on display. Turner answered the call. Listened. And was shocked to hear himself say, "Yeah, I'll be there."

It had been a voice from that thing he most wanted to avoid: the past. A time he remembered with the helpless yearning of a man who could not return to simpler things, simpler times, his simpler self.

But Cole Watson, his best friend from *before* Turner had ever known he had a gift for dealing with fear, had been trying to track him down for weeks. Said he needed him.

And Turner came from a world where one rule rose above all the others: when a buddy needed you, you were there.

Okay. So it wasn't a life-or-death request. No one's survival was on the line.

Cole was putting his life back in order. He'd lost nearly everything that mattered to him. He said he'd been given a second chance, and he planned to take it.

Was that the irresistible pull, then—second chances? It certainly wasn't a place in the back-woods of New England called the Gingerbread Inn, though the fact that Turner had never been there was a plus, as it held no memories.

No, Cole had casually mentioned that the inn sat on the shores of Barrow's Lake, where a man could put on his skates and go just about forever. That sounded like as good a way as any to spend the holiday season.

As good a way as any to deal with the energy that sang along Turner's nerve endings, begging for release. It sounded nearly irresistible.

CHAPTER ONE

CASEY CARAVETTA SIGHED with contentment.

"Being at the Gingerbread Inn with the two of you feels like being home," she said. She didn't add, *"in a way that home had never felt like."*

"Even with it being in such a state?" Emily asked, sliding a disapproving look around the front parlor. It was true the furniture was shabby, the paint was peeling, the rugs had seen better days.

"Don't you worry," Andrea said, "You are not going to recognize this place by the time I'm done with it. On Christmas Eve, Emily, for your vow renewal, the Gingerbread Inn will be transformed into the most amazing winter wonderland."

"I am so humbled that all the people Cole and I are closest to are going to give up their Christmas plans to be with us," Emily said.

"Nobody is giving up their Christmas plans," Andrea answered. "We're spending a magical Christmas Eve together, and then scattering to the four corners, to be wherever we need to be for Christmas."

Except Casey, who didn't need to be anywhere. And the inn, despite its slightly gone-to-seed appearance, would be the perfect place to spend a quiet day by herself.

The thought might have been depressing except for the gift Casey had decided to give herself....

Outside, snow had begun to fall, but the parlor's stone hearth held a fire that crackled merrily and threw a steady stream of glowing red sparks up the chimney.

Until she'd received Andrea's plea to take a little extra time off work and come to the Gingerbread Inn to make magic happen for Emily and Cole's renewal of vows, Casey had been looking forward to Christmas with about the same amount of anticipation she might have for a root canal.

In other words, the same as always.

Except, of course, for the gift, her secret plan to get her life back on track.

Now, here with her friends, cuddling her secret to her, Casey actually felt as if she might start humming, "It's beginning to feel a lot like Christmas...."

"That sense of home doesn't have a thing to do with looks," she said, wanting to share what she was feeling with her friends.

Belonging.

She had never felt it with her own family. At school, she had been the outsider, the too-smart geek. Her work was engrossing, but largely solitary.

But being here with Emily and Andrea, the Gingerbread Girls all together again, Casey felt hope.

Even though, sadly, Melissa was not here. Why did it take a tragedy for people to understand that friendship was a gift to be cherished, and not taken for granted?

Casey and Andrea had spent two days together here early in December, Casey seeking the refuge of friendship to try and outrun her latest family fiasco. Really, any given year she might as well block out all of December on her calendar and write "crisis" on it.

But before her meeting with Andrea it had been far too long since she and her friends, who'd always called themselves "the Gingerbread Girls," had been together.

After seeing Andrea, Casey had made her decision.

Now, she was loving the fact that they were as comfortable as if they had been together only yesterday. Sentences began with "Remember when..." and were followed by gales of laughter. The conversation flowed easily as they caught up on the details of one another's lives.

"Speaking of looks, I can't believe the way *you*

look," Emily told Casey for about the hundredth time. "I just can't get over it."

"You should be modeling," Andrea agreed.

"Modeling?" Casey laughed. "I think models are usually a little taller than five foot five."

"The world's loss," Andrea said with a giggle, and took a sip of her wine.

Casey sipped hers, as well. Emily, pregnant, her baby bump barely noticeable beneath her sweater, was glowing with happiness and was sipping sparkling fruit juice instead of wine.

Next year at this time, that could very well be me, Casey mused, and the thought made her giddy.

"How do you get your hair so straight?" Andrea asked. "You didn't have it like that when I saw you earlier this month. Remember how those locks of yours were the bane of your existence? All those wild curls. No matter what you did, that head of hair refused to be tamed. Remember the time we tried ironing it? With a clothes iron?"

Would her baby have wild curls? Casey hoped not.

"I always loved it," Emily said. "I was jealous."

"Of *my* hair?" she asked, incredulous. She touched it self-consciously. She had a flat iron that was state-of-the-art, a world away from what they had tried that humid summer day.

Still, her curls surrendered to the highest setting with the utmost reluctance, and were held at bay with enough gel to slide a 747 off a runway. And yet as she touched her hair, it felt coiled, ready to spring.

"I thought you were quite exotic, compared to Andrea and me."

"Really?"

"Why so surprised?"

Maybe it was her second glass of wine that made her admit it. "I always felt like the odd woman out. Here was this wonderful inn, out of an American dream, filled with all these wholesome families, like yours and Andrea's. And then there was the Caravetta clan. A boisterous Italian family, always yelling and fighting and singing and crying and laughing, and whatever we were doing, we were doing it loudly. Next to you and Andrea, I felt like I was a little too much of everything."

"But you weren't like that," Emily said. "You were always so quiet and contained. If you were too much of anything it was way too smart, Doc. Thinking all the time."

Casey dismissed the comment with a wave of her hand. "I didn't mean that. You were both tall, reed thin and fair, while I was short and plump, and had skin that came straight from the olive grove. You had well-behaved blond ponytails. I had dark tangles and coils that did whatever they wanted. You both have that all-American look, Emily, with your eyes like jade, and Andrea's like sapphires."

"There is nothing wrong with your eyes!" Andrea declared.

"Ha! My grandmother used to look at my eyes and say they were so dark she could see the devil in them. And then she'd cross herself."

Would Casey's baby have her eyes? Did she get to choose the eye color of the father? So much to learn!

"The devil? That's ridiculous, especially given how studious you were. But still, I always thought you were unusually striking, and faintly mysterious," Emily insisted.

"A model," Andrea reiterated. "I think you should be a model."

"A model," Casey snorted. "Believe me, I'm quite happy doing research at the lab."

"As noble as medical research is, Casey, isn't that a tad dull?" Emily asked.

"I love it," she said honestly. "I have such a sense of purpose to my days, a feeling I could make the world a better place."

"Isn't it a little, well, depressing? Childhood cancers?" Andrea pressed.

"My twin brother died of nasopharyngeal cancer when he was six," Casey said. *And so a family unravels.*

"I'd forgotten," Andrea said. "I'm so sorry."

"It was long before I met you," Casey said. "Don't worry about it." Out of the corner of her eye, she saw Emily give her little baby bump a protective pat. "And don't you worry about it, either. Childhood cancers are extremely rare," she assured her pregnant friend.

Casey was aware she might have chosen her work in some effort to make right all that had gone wrong in her family. But regardless of her motives, the order of science, after the unfolding chaos in her family, appealed to her. The wine hadn't, thankfully, loosened her tongue enough to tell them why she'd chosen the vow renewal over spending Christmas with her widowed mother.

"Maybe you could model on the side," Andrea said hopefully.

"Why would I want to?" Casey asked. "Talk about dull. Good grief. Hours on hair—" well, okay, her hair took nearly that long, anyway "—and makeup? I'd expire of pure boredom."

"Men," Andrea said knowingly. "You'd meet a zillion guys. How many do you meet in your dusty old lab?"

No sense pointing out there was not a speck of dust anywhere in her lab!

"And then," Andrea continued dreamily, "you could meet the right one. Look at how much Emily loves being married. Renewing her vows! And Rick and I will probably have a spring wedding. If you could find the perfect guy, all our kids could grow up together here in the summers, the same as we did."

How quickly things could change! Just a few weeks ago Andrea had been as determined not to fall in love as Casey herself was. Her friend was no weakling, so Casey inadvertently shivered at how love could overpower the most sensible of plans.

Emily shot Andrea a warning look that clearly said, *Careful, Casey is recovering from a broken heart*—last year's Christmas crisis. Then she tactfully tried to guide the conversation in a different direction. "Anyway, the inn is for sale."

Andrea appeared pained for a minute, but then shrugged it off. "I don't know. I've seen how Martin Johnson, the electrician, looks at Carol. I think he's a man capable of restoring the Gingerbread Inn to its former glory. And it seems it would be a labor of love."

"Carol is resisting him," Emily said. "I'm afraid I overheard a bit of a shouting match between them."

"Well, I'm going to help things along. I've already asked him to come and help with the lighting for the vow renewal, and he seemed very eager to say yes!"

"Good for you," Emily said, but doubtfully. "Honestly, while Cole and I were working things out we bonded over a few cosmetic repairs around the place, but every single thing we did has made us so aware of what else has to be done. Poor Carol, on her own, could not keep up. It may have deteriorated too badly to be saved."

They all sadly contemplated that.

The Gingerbread Inn was special. It always had been, and there could never be a replacement in Casey's heart. The walls held memories: laughter and love, families coming together. The ghosts of their younger selves played out there on the waters of Barrow's Lake, swimming, canoeing, sunning themselves on the dock, playing volleyball on the beach.

There would never be another place like the Gingerbread Inn. It was a refuge of simplicity in a complicated world.

"We could find a different place to spend family summers together," Andrea suggested tentatively. "Wherever it is, or whatever it is, the three of us will be there with our soul mates. I think that's what Melissa would have wanted us to learn. That this is what is important. Love. And I hope someday it will include all our babies. Babies who will grow into toddlers as love deepens all around us. Rick and I plan to adopt someday. Tessa would love a little brother or sister."

Tessa was the six-year-old who would become Andrea's stepdaughter. She was hands down the most adorable little girl on the planet.

"It's what I want for this baby, too," Emily said tenderly.

That old feeling of being the odd one out whispered along her spine, but Casey reminded herself she was not going to be that for long! But she was going to do things her way.

For as happy as both Emily and Andrea were now, Casey had been a bridesmaid at both their weddings. How those beautiful days had fuelled her longing for romance! But Andrea's dreams had ended in a terrible tragedy on her honeymoon. And Casey had seen the cracks appear in Emily's relationship almost before Emily had seen them herself.

Oh, sure, Emily and Cole were like lovers again *now,* and Andrea was still in the over-the-moon stage with her new love, Rick, but it was too late for Casey to believe in love.

The pain interwoven with the love in those relationships had just helped cement Casey's resolve to wrestle her weakest point to the ground. And that wasn't her hair, either!

"Well, you girls can believe in fairy tales if you want. I'm done with that," she announced.

"I've been there," Emily said sympathetically.

"Me, too," Andrea said. "But the old saying is true—it's darkest just before the dawn." Catching Emily's warning look, she added, "Okay. Casey doesn't have to be with someone. She could come by herself."

"Actually," Casey said slowly, her heart beating hard, "I may not be by myself."

If she told them it was like committing. Like carving it in stone. And yet who better to share this gloriously happy decision with than her best friends?

"What?" Andrea squealed. "Have you met someone new? Why did you let me prattle on about your dusty lab if you have? I'm so happy for you! Really, a year is quite long enough to recover from a rascal like Sebastian. I told you when I saw you earlier this month that eventually you would see your breakup as a blessing. And I am a testament to the fact that things can turn around in an absolute blink."

It had been a year, almost exactly, since the rather humiliating disintegration of her relationship. Only these two women knew all the details: how a coworker had tipped her off that her fiancé, Sebastian, was seeing another woman, only days before they were going to make a Christmas announcement of their engagement!

"I haven't exactly met someone," Casey said cautiously, suddenly feeling vulnerable about saying it out loud.

"What is going on, Casey?" Andrea asked. "You asked me to join you here earlier in the month because you were down, but now you look great. So who is he?"

"It's not a he. I've made a decision to give myself the most amazing gift."

"What?" her friends asked in unison.

"I'm going to have a baby. I'm going to start investigating third-party reproduction and cryobanks right after the holidays are over."

Her friends looked stunned. "Cryo what?" Emily asked weakly.

"You mean you're going to raise a child by yourself?" Andrea finally asked.

"Why not? I'm well established. I'm financially able to afford the procedures. I'm ready. I think, on my own, I could provide as stable a family as most I've seen."

"That seems very scientific," Emily ventured. "Procedure as a way to make a baby?"

"I am a scientist!" And really, science had given her far more than her family ever had. "I'm done with romantic love. I'm saving all my love for my baby."

Her friends were very quiet.

"Hey," Casey said, trying for humor, when she was really disappointed they weren't more supportive of her decision. "You're both so serious. I said I was done with love, and that there could be a baby in my future, not that I was going to burn the Gingerbread Inn down!"

"You couldn't," Andrea said with dreamy satisfaction. "Rick would rescue it."

Rick, the adorable Tessa's father, was a fireman.

"I'm curing myself of romantic notions. I'm tackling my fatal flaw," Casey surprised herself by announcing.

"Your fatal flaw?" Andrea said, frowning.

"I believed in romantic love," Casey said. "Worse, I believed in love at first sight. It's done nothing but cause me grief, and I'm done with it."

"Love at first sight?" Emily said, puzzled. "I thought you and Sebastian worked together for some time before you agreed to go out with him."

But her secret, even from Em and Andrea, was that Sebastian had not been her first love. Her first love she had loved at first sight. He was the one who had made her so foolishly long for love that she had been willing to overlook her own family's history with passion, and imbue her former fiancé with characteristics he did not have.

"I'm done with love," Casey repeated, even more firmly than before.

"You are not!" Emily said, dismayed. "How can anybody just be done with love?"

"We buried Melissa," Casey said. "That's enough all by itself."

"I understand how you feel," Andrea said softly. "After Gunter died I wanted to give up on love, too. But I'm so glad I didn't."

Though Casey could not say it, the death of Andrea's husband—on their honeymoon, no less—felt like part of her disillusionment. Giving your heart was a risky business.

"No one would be more appalled than Melissa if you made fear of love her legacy!"

The Gingerbread Girls had always bowed to Emily's leadership, and Casey conceded slightly now. "Okay. This kind of love I'm fine with. The bonds between friends. The love between a mother and a child. Romantic love I'm done with. *Finis.*"

"I always love it when you speak Italian," Andrea said, deciding in the face of Casey's intensity it was time to lighten up.

"It's Latin," she said. "Not Italian."

Andrea rolled her eyes at the correction and went on as if she had not been interrupted. "You aren't done with it. You're hurting right now. But it has been a year, and I think you have healed more than you think you have. You are planning on having a baby, after all. Though I do wish you'd wait for the right guy to come along, and spadoodle, life as you know it, over."

"Spadoodle?" Casey laughed in spite of herself.

"I thought it sounded Italian," Andrea offered with an impish grin.

"Sort of," Emily said, as if she was considering. "Like *spaghetti* and *noodle* mixed." And then they were all laughing, like the carefree girls they had once been. It felt again like a homecoming, it was so good to be with them.

"I agree with Andrea, though. The right guy will come along and you'll see that every single thing about your life, including the parts that seem bad, were getting you ready for that moment," Emily said. "Should you put off having a baby until that happens? Really, I know that's not for me to say."

Casey felt her friend was not entirely approving and had decided to keep it light, and she was grateful for that.

"From spadoodle to deep philosophy in the blink of an eye?" Casey said, lightly. "It's enough to make my head spin."

Emily grinned. "Way too deep, eh, Doc?"

"Way," Casey said with an answering smile, and it all seemed okay again. Her decision to come here had been a good one. The sisterhood between them that allowed them to squabble and exchange confidences and well-meaning advice, and then just rest in pure love and laughter again, was balm to her soul.

"I wish you'd give love a chance," Andrea insisted.

"I have given love a chance," Casey said firmly. "What's that old saying? If you always do what you've always done, you'll always get what you always got. Falling in love, for me, equals heartbreak. And I'm not doing it anymore."

"You sound sure of yourself," Emily mused.

"I am."

"Maybe Andrea's right. Maybe you've spent too

much time in the lab and it has given you this illusion about what you can control. Maybe before you fully commit to the idea of having a baby on your own, you should try getting out a bit."

"I'm getting out. I've joined yoga! And I'm taking a calligraphy class. My life is exceedingly full."

She inwardly begged Andrea not to mention that desperate call a few weeks ago when she had been so unbearably down.

Andrea, blessedly, didn't.

But Emily said, "Full does not mean fulfilling."

"That's why I want a family of my own. Besides, when did you become such a philosopher? Now you two quit picking on me."

"I'm sorry," Emily said, "I didn't mean to pick on you. If this decision makes you happy, I'm happy for you."

Casey just wanted to change the subject. "Andrea, tell me what I should get the adorable little Tessa for Christmas. I was thinking a nice chemistry set."

They all laughed, and it didn't take much of a shove to get Andrea talking about her new life and her new family. "I've already tucked away the giant gingerbread man Tessa fell in love with at the shop."

Andrea went on to talk about what she was getting Rick. She was glowing with passion, that thing that Casey was most suspicious of.

Both her friends knew what a philanderer her father had been. He'd no doubt made moves on both their mothers at some time over the summers here! And when her own mom had found out? Shrieking and pot throwing and breaking glass.

And then passion clouding the poor woman's judgment all over again.

"How is your mother since your father passed?" Andrea asked suddenly, as if she had picked it up telepathically. Such was the way between old friends.

You don't want to know. "Fine," Casey said briefly.

"I wish she would come for the vow renewal," Emily said. "She's not going to be alone because you've come here, is she?"

"Oh, no," Casey managed to squeak. "She's not going to be alone."

She could feel her throat tightening suspiciously, and she swallowed hard and focused quickly on the inn's dog, a gorgeous golden retriever mix named Harper. The female dog came up with her happy grin and put her head in Casey's lap.

"This kind of love I can live with," Casey said lightly, scratching the dog's ears and smiling at the tail thumping on the floor. "Oh, look! It's snowing."

She gently maneuvered free of the affectionate pet, then got up and went to the window. She shouldn't have told her friends she had given up on love. Maybe she shouldn't have told them she was thinking of alternative ways to have a family, either. She had left herself wide-open to a Christmas campaign to make her change her mind.

But she'd had enough proof of the folly of love to last her a lifetime, and it should be easy enough to change the subject when it came up.

As she looked out the window, headlights illuminated the thickly falling snow. A cab emerged from the night and pulled up in front of the inn, sliding a little when it tried to stop on the icy driveway.

A man got out of the back, dressed casually in a parka with a fur-lined hood, jeans tucked into laced snow boots. He strode around to the rear and waited for the driver to retrieve his bags from the trunk. Then, with his luggage at his feet in the snow, he paid the cabbie, clapping him on the shoulder at his effusive thanks for what must have been a great Christmas tip.

It was dark and it was snowing hard, but there was something about the way the new arrival carried himself that penetrated both the storm and the night.

Something shivered along Casey's spine.

She had the alarming feeling it might be recognition, but she shook it off.

It simply was not possible that, following so

quickly on her announcement to her friends that she had sworn off love, Turner Kennedy—the first man who had ever stolen her heart—would show up here.

CHAPTER TWO

"DID SOMEBODY JUST arrive?" Andrea asked. "Another member of my little work party?"

"I thought *we* were your little work party," Casey said, trying not to panic. "Emily and me."

"Well, you were, but Cole pointed out to me he doesn't want Emily to do any heavy lifting, and he didn't really think you would want to be up on the roof replacing strings of Christmas lights. He wanted another guy, even though I asked Martin to help with the electrical. He said he'd be happy to do it for nothing. Isn't that nice?"

Casey was having trouble focusing on Martin's niceness.

"Who is it?" Emily asked. "He wouldn't tell me who he invited. He just said it would be a surprise. I'm guessing Joe."

"I'm not sure who it is," Casey said, though she was guessing it was not Joe! She was amazed at how normal her voice sounded, considering she was forcing words out past constricted vocal chords. Because if it was who she suspected, it was a surprise, all right. Of the worst possible sort!

And why wouldn't Turner Kennedy be just the surprise Cole would bring to the inn? the scientist in Casey insisted on asking. It was certainly one of the available options!

Turner had been the best man at Emily and Cole's wedding. Why wouldn't he be here as they assembled as much of the original wedding party as was possible for their renewal of vows? Why wouldn't he jump at the chance to help get the old inn ready for their magical day, just as she had?

Because he disappeared, Casey wailed to herself.

Still, at one time, he and Cole had been best friends. Casey had assumed the friendship had been left behind, because when she had asked—not nearly as frequently as she wanted to, and with only the most casual interest—Emily had been vague.

"Oh. I'll have to ask Cole. I think he said Turner is overseas. He's some kind of government contractor."

She'd thought, in those three magical days they had spent together following the wedding, that they had known everything about each other. Government contractor? Casey had felt the first shiver of betrayal at that. He hadn't mentioned anything about being a government contractor. But in retrospect, he *had* headed her off every single time she had tried to delve into his life.

Just pretend I'm a prince who found a glass slipper. And that it fits you.

"If Turner is somewhere amazing, like France or Italy," Emily had said, thankfully not reading her friend's distress, "Cole and I should go visit!"

And when, after waiting an appropriate amount of time, Casey had screwed up the nerve to ask if Emily had asked Cole about Turner, her friend had replied, "Cole said he's lost touch. Men! Relationships are a low priority."

That was actually the first time Casey had heard bitterness in Emily's voice in reference to her busy husband. But not the last.

Why would Turner be here now? Well, why not?

Why wouldn't he come and help celebrate Christmas with his best friend's newly reunited and rejoicing family? It went with everything Emily had been saying about the changes Cole was making. Her husband was giving a new priority to building and keeping relationships.

That's what Casey was doing, too, wasn't it? Making a vow to realize the importance of friendships before it was too late? Celebrating Christmas and the spirit of love with her best friends instead of that crazy, unpredictable, painful conglomeration of people sometimes known as a family?

Even her decision to create the kind of family

she had always wanted for herself seemed to be wavering, perhaps due to some combination of her friends' lack of enthusiasm and his arrival.

Stop it, Casey ordered herself. She didn't even know if it was Turner. But all the ordering in the world would not slow her heart as the cab pulled away, and the man bent, effortlessly picked up a duffel bag and looped the strap over his shoulder, before turning to the steps that led to the front porch.

Casey was aware she was holding her breath as he stepped toward the faint light being thrown by a string of Christmas lights with too many burned out bulbs.

The light may have been weak, but it washed the familiar contours of his face, and turned the snowflakes caught in the glossy darkness of his hair to gold.

Her gasp was audible, and she covered it with quick desperation by clearing her throat. Casey's wineglass trembled in her hand. She set it down. She told herself to move, to get out of here *fast*.

Instead, she was glued to the spot, her feet frozen, her eyes locked on his face.

It was him.

It was Turner. It was Turner Kennedy in the flesh.

Not unchanged, though the changes were subtle. Something in the way he held himself made a

CARA COLTER   37

shiver go up and down her spine. As he arrived at
the bottom of the step, he paused.

He had broadened in the years since she had
last seen him, youthful litheness giving way to the
pure power of a man completely in his prime. What
hadn't changed was that he was exuding an almost
sizzling sense of himself, who he was in the world,
and what he could take on.

Anything.

If the door of the inn had suddenly crashed open
and a horde of bandits had fallen upon him, she
had the sense he would be ready for it. He might
even enjoy it!

Casey shook the picture off, annoyed that she
could be so susceptible to the whisper of imagina-
tion. She knew nothing about him. She had once
convinced herself otherwise, and she had been
wrong.

The faint light illuminated his face, and she shivered again, despite herself. There seemed to be a
certain remoteness in his expression that was different, but what did she know? She'd been a naive
young bridesmaid when Turner Kennedy had been
Cole Watson's best man.

She had been the geeky girl, the science nerd, the
brain, who had been noticed by the most popular
boy in the school, the captain of the football team,
the boy whose picture in every girl's yearbook was
marked with inked hearts.

Despite his closed expression, Turner was still the most astonishingly handsome man she had ever seen, so good-looking that a girl could fall for him.

At first sight.

So much so that when he had taken her chin in his hands as dawn broke, the morning after Cole and Emily's wedding, and said, "Run away with me," she hadn't even hesitated.

Casey had tossed years and years of absolute control right out the window.

"Three days," he'd said. "Spend the next three days with me."

She should have known better than to share her new resolve about love with her girlfriends. It seemed she had thrown a gauntlet before the gods and they had responded with terrifying swiftness.

"Casey?"

She turned to her friends and saw the instant concern register on both their faces.

"What's wrong?" they asked together.

What's wrong? She was a scientist. Andrea had been right; she spent too much time in the lab. And nothing in that carefully controlled environment had prepared her for this encounter.

She was amazed when her voice didn't shake when she said, "It looks like Turner Kennedy is here."

"Turner?" Emily said. "I can't believe it! We haven't

seen him since our wedding. I thought Cole had lost touch completely."

Emily got up, raced to the front door and flung it open. "Turner Kennedy! What a wonderful surprise!"

Casey was experiencing that trapped feeling, a sensation of fight or flight. When Andrea went into the front hallway to greet the newcomer, too, Casey quietly set down her unfinished wineglass, left the parlor by the back door and slipped up the rear staircase to her room.

She went in and softly closed the door, leaning against it as if she had escaped a twisting, foggy London street with the Ripper on her heels.

Her heart was beating hard and unreasonably fast, not entirely the result of her mad dash up the stairs.

She turned and looked at her suitcase.

Good. Not completely unpacked yet. She could throw the few things she had unpacked back in it. She could wait in here, quiet as a mouse, until the old inn grew silent, and then slink out that door and never come back.

She could spend a quiet Christmas in her apartment. Never mind that she had yearned for the company of loving friends. Never mind that she had longed for holiday traditions, for bonfires and impromptu snowball fights, hanging stockings on the hearth and making gingerbread cookies with the

Gingerbread Girls. Never mind that she had longed for a little taste of the kind of Christmas she would create for her own child someday soon!

Never mind all that. She would go to her little apartment, where it was safe and everything was in her control. She could look up everything she needed to know about third-party reproductive procedures.

Maybe she'd even go to the lab for part of Christmas Day. Why not?

Her research there could be her greatest gift to the world. Ask any parent whose child had been diagnosed with cancer!

Another option would be to accept her mother's invitation.

To join her at the Sacred Heart Mission House, where the Sisters of Mercy would be serving Christmas dinner to the poor. Where her mother, glowing with a soft joy she had never had while Casey was growing up, would remind her, ever so gently, not to call her Mom.

It's Sister Maria Celeste.

There. Both the Caravettas—except her mother did not consider herself a Caravetta any longer—selflessly saving the world at Christmas.

Her crazy family, the reason Casey had sought refuge with her friends at the inn.

But she couldn't stay here now.

It was one thing to say you were sworn off romantic love. It was another to be tested.

And Turner Kennedy had that indefinable *something* that would test any woman's resolve, never mind one who had been locked away in a lab nursing a broken heart for nearly a year.

Or had it been longer? Had it really been ever since that three days together in a fairy-tale kingdom he had created? Just for her. A Cinderella experience. The little scrub-a-muffin noticed by the prince. The prince enchanted with her.

Only in the end, the fairy tale had been reversed. He had been the one with secrets. The one who had resisted her every effort to find out why only three days, where he was going, what he would be doing next. He had been the one who had disappeared into the night, only unlike the fairy tale, Turner had not left a single clue.

She had been left holding a memory as fragile as a glass slipper, only she had never again found the person who fit it.

But now he was here. Yes, Turner had a raw masculine potency combined with a roguish, boyish charm that had completely bowled her over on their first encounter.

Casey turned off the lights in her room and lay on her bed, staring at the glow of the mostly burned out string of Christmas lights outside her window. They were making a really ugly pattern on her waterstained ceiling. She contemplated how the hurt Turner had caused her felt recent, more recent than the hurt of her broken engagement!

In a different part of the house, she could hear everyone's voices, Cole's and Turner's, raised in greeting, followed by laughter and conversation. She could, after all these years, pick out the tone of Turner's voice. It was deep, a masculine melody touching the harp her spine had become.

It was obvious the men were now in the front room where the Gingerbread Girls had been earlier.

No chance of sneaking down the staircase without being seen. Casey fervently wished they would shut up and go to bed, so she could get out of here.

Instead, Turner's voice triggered powerful memories of a presidential suite at the Waldorf Astoria. Jumping on the beds. Sitting in front of the fireplace wrapped in a luxurious, pure white robe, while he painted her toenails red. Walking to the theater. Taking a carriage ride through Central Park.

Three days of barely sleeping, of living with an intensity that was exhilarating and exhausting, of being on fire with life and love… Strip away all the luxury, and it was his hand in hers that had caused her to feel so exquisitely alive, his eyes on her face that made her feel as if she had never felt before.

Enough! Casey shook her head clear of the memories. Finally, after experiencing what she had once seen described in a poem as the "interminable night," she felt it was safe to creep out of her room, jacket on against the cold, suitcase in hand.

She checked the hallway. Nothing. Not a sound beyond the wheezing of an exceptionally cranky old furnace. She was pretty sure Harper slept with her owner, the innkeeper, Carol.

Casey tiptoed through the house and out the front, where the screen door shrieked like a cat whose tail had been stepped on.

She froze, listened, waited for lights to come on. It was really dark out here. Even the Christmas lights had been turned off, no doubt part of the Gingerbread Inn's austerity program.

Stumbling through the inky darkness found only in the country, Casey finally made it to her car, where she opted to use the key so there would be no blink of headlights or short blast of the horn when she unlocked it. She actually had her key in the door when it hit her.

She could not let Emily and Andrea down like this. It wasn't about her. It was about making Emily's day the most incredible experience of her life.

Besides, what explanation could she offer to her friends for her sudden defection? As close as she was to them, she had never let on about those three days she and Turner had spent together. Had never breathed out loud that she harbored a crush on the man, that she had waited and hoped and prayed that he would contact her again.

The memory of that—of waiting—made her cheeks turn crimson with anger.

She was acting like a thief! Acting as if *she* had done something wrong.

It was Turner who had breathed fire into her soul in those three days that had followed Cole and Emily's wedding. And then he had walked away, and never, ever called. Or written. Had disappeared as if they had not shared the most intense of all experiences.

As if they had not fallen in love at first sight.

Slowly, she pulled her key out of the car door.

Casey was a scientist. She didn't believe in the phenomena of coincidence, certainly did not believe in the universe conspiring to help people out. But really, in terms of her vow never to love again, could there be a more perfect test than this?

Could there be a better conclusion than coming face-to-face with the man who had made her aware of her fatal flaw?

It was perfect, really.

The perfect ending.

Not the one Andrea and Emily wanted her to believe in. No, in this story, the princess was not kissed awake by a prince. In this ending, the princess came awake all by herself. In her new happily-ever-after, Casey would walk away, sure of herself, entirely certain of her ability to be completely independent, to live with purpose and joy without being encumbered by a belief in the fairy-tale ending of love.

Love, even love that worked, was an uphill battle with heartache. Look at Em. Look at Andrea, having to bury her husband before her honeymoon had even ended!

Casey decided—right then and there, in the parking lot of the Gingerbread Inn, with fresh snow drifting down around her—to be on a quest, not for love, but for emotional freedom. She would rid herself once and for all of the lifelong myths and fantasies and hopes and dreams that had bound and imprisoned her.

Her life would be about her baby. Who better than a scientist to conduct the search for a donor with the perfect qualities to give her child?

She could make that decision about creating her own family in the way all the best choices were made. She would be measured and rational. She hadn't got far in her research about how to choose a donor, but she hoped she would get to review photos. She would make sure the father of her child was nothing like her own devastatingly handsome father had been, or her immensely charming, but ultimately fickle fiancé.

The man would, especially, be nothing like Turner.

Who could turn those silvery eyes on a woman and enchant her entirely.

No, better to look for brilliance and gentleness, physical health and even features.

Really, she was surprised she hadn't thought of it sooner—that science could provide her with a perfect father for her children!

When she thought back on it, she was a totally different woman than she had been in those few long-ago days with Turner.

She'd experienced nothing but heartache at the caprice of love. She'd buried her father, lost her fiancé to another woman and her mother to the church, attended the heartbreaking funeral of one of her best friends. She'd seen Andrea devastated by the death of her husband, and Emily by a struggling marriage. It was enough! Casey's heart was in armor.

She was glad that Emily and Andrea had found love. She really was. But she was concluding her mission. The rejection of romantic love would make her a better mother to her future child, devoted and not distracted. Their lives wouldn't be in a constant jumble of men moving in and out.

If the gods were throwing down a gauntlet in the face of her decision, she was accepting the challenge!

And with that firmly in mind, Casey grasped the handle of her suitcase and turned back to the inn with a certain grim determination. She plowed through the growing mounds of snow and marched up the steps onto the covered porch.

Something wet and cold brushed the hand that held her car keys. Casey dropped them with a little shriek of surprise, then looked down to see Harper thrust a wet snout into her palm.

"What are you doing out here?" she asked the dog.

A deep voice, as sensual as the snow-filled night, came out of a darkened corner of the porch.

"Keeping me company."

CHAPTER THREE

CASEY SHRIEKED EVEN more loudly than she had when the dog had thrust its wet, cold snout into her hand.

She dropped her suitcase from nerveless fingers, and it landed with a thump beside her keys. The suitcase was an old one with a hard shell, and to her horror, the latch popped and the lid flew open, displaying her neatly packed underthings.

Right on top were embarrassingly lacy garments she would no longer be needing now that she had decided to move procreation into the controllable field of science, rather than the uncontrollable one of attraction.

The dog shoved her head forward as if about to follow her instincts and retrieve.

Casey squatted down and slammed the lid, nearly catching Harper's snout. The dog whined, perplexed at being thwarted, then while Casey struggled with the sticky latch, she noticed the keys.

"Harper," Casey pleaded, "don't—"

With a happy thump of her tail, the dog scooped up the keys. Holding them in her mouth as gently as she would have a downed bird, she delivered them to the shadowy figure in the darkness of the porch, forcing Casey, finally, to look at him.

Harper sat down, tail thumping, offering him the prize.

"Keys," he said, in the voice that played music on Casey's harp.

He took them, examined them, jingling them with a certain satisfaction.

"To the chambers of a lovely maiden? What a good dog. So much better than a newspaper or slippers."

It was said with the ease of a man comfortable with his attraction, confident in how women reacted to him. Luckily for Casey, her guard was up. Way up. And luckily for her, she was intensely wary of men who were so smoothly sure of themselves!

Gathering her composure—it was a test of the gods, after all—she straightened, turned and glared in his direction.

His voice was deep and faintly sardonic. She tried to ignore the fact it felt as if his words had vibrated along the nape of her neck, as sensual as the scrape of fingertips.

Turner Kennedy was sitting on the railing that surrounded the covered porch, one foot resting on the floor, the other up, swinging ever so slightly as he watched her.

He had a cigarette in his hand, but it wasn't lit.

She detested men who smoked. Which was a good thing. Coupled with his flirtatious remark, and the fact he had scared her nearly to death, Turner was at strike three already, and she had shared the porch with him for barely fifteen seconds.

Still, a part of her insisted on remembering he had not smoked back then.

Good grief! It had been years ago. He hadn't smoked then, but they were both different people by now! She had been tried, tested and spit out by life since then. Plus she wasn't a callow, stars-in-her-eyes girl any longer. She was a respected member of an important research team.

How long had he been there? Had he seen her exit the inn with determination, stumble through the darkness, put her key in the car door, only to come back with just as much determination?

Casey wanted to escape, dash in the front door of the Gingerbread Inn without another word. Over her shoulder she could give instructions for him to leave her keys on the table on the front entryway.

But that was childish. And that was not why she had come back. Her responses to him seemed very primal—flight or fight.

She was going to have to see him sometime. She

was rattled, but she was not letting that show! She was ready to fight!

She had run from him once tonight, and she was not doing it again. Casey ignored the hammering of her heart and forced down her clamoring insecurities. She crossed the distance between them with all the confidence of the successful, purposeful woman she had become since their last meeting.

This was an opportunity to face her demons head-on. To rid herself of the pull of such men, so that she could be a better mother. Her own mother would say that such a coincidence was heaven sent, though as a scientist Casey didn't believe in such things.

Smiling faintly, Turner watched her come.

He had been exceptional looking all those years ago: dark-chocolate hair, eyes the color of pewter, high proud cheekbones, straight nose, strong chin, sensual full lips. Now, he had matured into something even finer.

Though the night was frosty, his jacket was hanging over the railing beside him. Underneath a beautifully tailored dress shirt—a deep shade of walnut that set off the silver of his eyes—his shoulders were unbelievably broad, his chest deep. Casey could tell there was not an ounce of superfluous flesh on him. The shirt was open at the throat and he had rolled up the sleeves to just below his elbows. His forearms were corded with strength.

She could actually feel some masculine power heat the cool air around him as he gazed at her, that smile lifting one corner of his sexy mouth. He was a man who was way too sure of himself.

"Just keys," she said, "to an ordinary room. Not a suite at the Waldorf." She held out her hand for them.

The Waldorf Astoria with Casey Caravetta. When Turner had been lured here by the promise of endless ice, he hadn't really thought of that.

Of who else might be here. He certainly had not thought *she* would be.

Casey had been a bridesmaid at Emily and Cole's wedding. Turner had been the best man. Unknown to anyone, even his best friend, he had been on countdown.

The newly formed and top secret Tango unit had been shipping out on their first mission four days after the wedding.

Maybe it had been that heightened awareness that had made him see Casey in an entirely different light than he usually would have.

They had spent the night of the wedding together—and not in the way he was used to spending nights with young women. She wasn't, after all, his regular kind of girl.

She had been almost comically uptight at first. Geeky and sweet. With just the tiniest nudge, she had poured out her heart to him. Her walls had come down and revealed a young woman who was brilliant and funny and deep. And damaged by life.

He'd found himself unable to say good-night, and feeling compelled to give her something. A break from herself—from the rigid control she exercised over herself. He wanted her to have some carefree, no-strings-attached fun, a taste of the life-lit-from-within intensity that predeployment was making him feel.

He'd had the means to do it. Settlements from his father's death had left him with a whole pile of money that he wanted to get rid of. What if he used it to do something good?

He'd had four days before he flew off to an uncertain future. Everyone who signed up for Tango knew they were in for highly dangerous work. With no guarantee they were ever coming back.

It had been like adopting a little sister.

Except, before the days had come to an end, he had not been feeling very brotherly toward her. Looking at her now, he could remember jumping on the bed at the Waldorf, and painting her toenails, and laughing until his stomach hurt. He could remember the feel of her hand in his, the light that had shone, wondrous, in her eyes, the break from a self-imposed discipline that had made him crush the fullness of her lips beneath his own on the final night....

* * *

As Casey watched recognition darken Turner's eyes, his smile faded. But not before she had noted teeth that were as white as the snow that fell around them. They drew Casey's gaze, unwillingly, to the sinful sexiness of that mouth.

But it was not the smile she remembered. The one she recalled had been boyish and open. Now, despite his flirtatious tone, and the faint smile, she could see something ever so subtly guarded in him.

She met his eyes, and again noted a change. The once clear gray held shadows, like frozen water reflecting storm clouds.

She frowned. Her memory, from those days together after Cole and Emily's wedding, was of eyes that sparked with carefree mischief.

Turner's eyebrows edged up. He threw the cigarette away and got down off the railing.

He reached out with his right hand and touched, ever so lightly, the hollow of her throat.

"I did scare you," he said apologetically. "Your heart is beating like that of a doe trapped against a fence by wolves."

More like a deer in the headlights, because though she ordered herself to slap his hand away, she stood absolutely paralyzed by his touch. His fingers radiated a stunningly sensual warmth on the cold of her neck.

Still, by sheer force of will, she managed to keep

her expression neutral. Better he think her heart was pounding like that from being startled, rather than from seeing him again.

Unfortunately, she wasn't sure which it was, especially with his merest touch causing a riot of sensation within her. Which it was best he not know about, as well!

So, telling herself it was completely her choice, Casey didn't move, not even when his hand drifted briefly to her hair and rested there for a deliciously suspended moment in time.

"Casey Caravetta," he said, his voice gruff, his hand dropping away. "No, wait. I'm sure I heard it was Dr. Caravetta now. Congratulations."

How was it that he had heard things about her when she had heard nothing about him? Not even a whisper.

She felt just like that young bridesmaid again. The geeky girl who had been noticed by the most amazingly attractive man she had ever laid eyes on.

His touch on the pulse at her throat had been soft, hardly a touch at all. Why did it feel as if a mark were burned into her skin?

This was what she was fighting, Casey reminded herself. And really, she was armed with the knowledge now that it was nothing but chemistry: serotonin, oxytocin, adrenaline, dopamine, a system flooded with intoxication. Attraction was the pure and simple science of a brain wired to recreate the

SNOWFLAKES AND SILVER LININGS

human race, but of course, it was way more palpable to people if it disguised itself as romance. She was a scientist; she should know better. She was a scientist and science had provided more convenient ways to have children.

But somehow it was not a scientist that watched as Turner ran his hand through his thick, glossy hair. Snow had melted in it, and little drops flew off as he did so.

She never looked away from him, and was astounded again at the stern lines that bracketed a mouth she remembered quirking upward with good humor and boyish charm.

She had to gain control of herself! She had to remind herself—and him—about the painful past between them.

"Are you just going to pretend you didn't ditch me at the Waldorf Astoria?" she asked. She hoped for a cool note, but could hear her own fury.

"I didn't ditch you," he said, genuinely perplexed. "You always knew I was going. I told you right from the beginning—three days."

"And on the morning of the fourth day, I woke up in that huge suite by myself! You didn't even have the decency to say goodbye."

His eyes rested on her lips. "I said it the night before." His voice was like gravel. Was it remembrance of that final kiss—the leashed passion in it—causing that slightly hoarse note?

"Humph." Did she have to sound like a disgruntled schoolmarm?

"It's not as if we were parting lovers, Casey. You were innocent then, and despite the showy underwear—"

He *had* seen! Casey could only pray the darkness of the porch would hide the fact her cheeks probably matched the underwear at the moment!

"—I bet not much has changed. I take back the remark about keys and chambers. Sheesh. I feel like I've propositioned a nun."

She flinched, and he jammed his hands in the pockets of his jeans.

"Sorry," he muttered. "I didn't mean that I don't find you—"

"Stop!" she said. She did not want to hear all the reasons why she was not the girl for him. He'd already made that more than plain.

"I wasn't offended," she said quickly, her tone deliberately icy. Well, maybe she was. A little. But he certainly didn't have to know that. "I'm just a little sensitive on the topic of nuns right now."

His lips twitched. "That hasn't changed. You have this way of saying things that is refreshing and funny."

"I wasn't trying to be funny," she said, annoyed.

Her annoyance had the unfortunate effect of deepening his amusement.

"I know you weren't trying to be funny, but that's

part of what makes it so. I mean, who is sensitive on the topic of nuns? Right now? It would be like me saying, 'I'm sensitive to the topic of Attila the Hun. Right now.'"

"The comparison only works if I mentioned Attila the Hun in reference to you. Which I didn't."

Rather than getting her point, he deepened his smile.

"Dr. Caravetta," he said, "you are funny, even if unintentionally. And brilliant. So, what makes you sensitive to the topic of nuns? Right now?"

His lips were twitching, but his own amusement seemed to catch him off guard, as if he was not easily amused by much anymore. Was that why he contained it before it fully bloomed, or was it because he caught on she was not sharing his amusement?

"It's a long story, and one I am not prepared to go into in the middle of the night." *Or ever.*

"Okay," he said. "Just to set the record straight, I wouldn't have made that crack about the key to your chambers if I'd known it was you. Really. It feels as if you're my best friend's little sister."

"Which I am not! I'm not even remotely related to Cole."

"Logically, I know that. At a different level, you have this quality of innocence that makes me feel protective of you. Even after a glimpse of the flashy underwear. I mean you are, by your own admission, the kind of girl who is sensitive to nuns."

Flashy underwear? Protective of her? Little sister? Casey was being flooded with fight-or-flight chemistry again, because she had a very uncharacteristic desire to smack that smirk right off his face!

Her memories of those days together were of electricity, of feeling like a woman for the first time in her life. Of acknowledging a deep and primal hunger within her that only one thing would fill. Her memories of those days were of being on fire with wanting.

For him. For this man.

Who probably set off that very same chemical reaction in every single female he came in contact with!

But for the entire three days they had spent together, he had stopped short, way short, of anything that would have fulfilled that wanting. Yes, they had kissed on that final night—the memory made it feel as if that pulse in her throat was hammering harder—but he, not she, had put on the brakes. It was Turner who had sent her into the other bedroom, on those rare occasions when they had given in and slept.

She felt they had connected so deeply on so many levels.

She had been convinced at a soul level.

While he'd been thinking it felt as if she was his best friend's little sister!

No wonder, with the dawn of the fourth day, he had disappeared, never to be seen or heard from again.

Now, as well as seeing her as his best friend's little sister, he was going to think of nuns when he saw her? Which, of course, was better than him thinking of flashy underwear. Wasn't it?

"Don't act as if you know anything about me on the basis of three days of acquaintance," Casey said tightly, "because you don't."

If he mentioned the underwear, she was going to die.

Of course he mentioned the underwear.

"But I do," he said softly. "I know that, despite the undies, the only thing wild about you is your hair. Or at least it used to be." He lifted his hand as if he was going to touch her again, and then drove it into his pocket instead. "Now it's not even that."

"I'll repeat," she said, with a coolness she was far from feeling, "you don't know anything about me."

"I know I liked your hair better the way it used to be."

"That's about you," she pointed out. "What *you* like."

"You're right," he said, cocking his head, considering her. "I am an accurate representative of the colossal self-centeredness of the male beast."

It seemed to her that her underwear should have intrigued a healthy male beast, at the very least, not been dismissed out of hand!

"But those curls," he added, mournfully. "It was as if a gypsy dancer was trapped inside of you, champing to get out."

It was still faintly dismissive, as if he found her funny rather than sexy. He, the one who had touched his lips to hers, and very nearly set that gypsy free!

But, thank goodness, he hadn't unleashed that family legacy of passion in her. Still, the silly girl in her who wanted to preen at his admiration of her hair had to be quashed. Immediately.

So did the gypsy inside her who had, after all, chosen that underwear, and who knew *exactly* how to erase little sisters and nuns from his mind in association with her.

An insane image materialized in her brain. Of her shocking him. Of her being the kind of woman who could pull off sexy red lace. Of her taking one step forward, capturing his lips, kissing him until he was begging her not to stop, but to go on.

Casey wrestled her multiple personalities into submission and held out her hand. "My keys?"

He dangled them above her waiting palm, but didn't let go. When he looked at her, his gaze steady and stripping, she was shocked that she felt astoundingly the same as she had felt all those years ago.

As if he truly saw her. As if he saw things about her no one else ever had. As if he knew everything and anything there was to know about her that was of any interest at all! But she'd been so much more naive back then than she was now.

Now she knew some men just had a gift—an intensity, a power of focus—that could make a woman feel as if she was the only one in his world.

"Is Christmas still the hardest thing for you?" he asked, softly.

Oh, no. There was seeing underthings, and then there was seeing under things.

"W-w-what would make you say that?"

"You told me. You told me that your twin brother died on Christmas Day. Angelo," Turner said softly.

Her best friends had not remembered this. Did Emily and Andrea even know her brother's name?

"I remember," he continued softly, "that you told me how you so wanted a Christmas miracle, and prayed for one. How you bargained with God. And Santa Claus. *'Just let my brother live.'* That stuck with me.

"And when I heard you'd gone into medical research, it was, like, *you go, girl.* You *make* your miracle happen. If any such thing exists, I hope you are the one who gets it."

He looked hard at her, and she had a feeling she

was not hiding the tears that pressed from behind her eyes.

"I'm sorry," he said. "I probably shouldn't have mentioned that. I'm turned around. I'm somewhere between exhausted and delirious."

"How could I get a miracle?" she demanded softly. "No matter how my research goes, I can't bring back my brother."

"Not that I consider myself anything of an expert on miracles—" he laughed slightly, a deeply cynical sound "—but it seems to me it's something of one that you are determined to turn your own loss into something good for someone else."

Casey realized it was this exact thing she had run from when she had headed for her car in the deep, dark night instead of wanting to chance an encounter with him.

It felt as if Turner *saw* her, went straight past the red lace to the core of her, and went to it with alarming swiftness.

This was the same way she had felt during those three days together.

As if, for the first time in her life, someone had seen her. As if, for the first time in her life, she was not completely alone.

But that was why she was at the beginning stages of making her plan to create her own family, to have a baby.

So that she would not be so alone anymore. And

so she did not have to rely on someone who had proved himself as unreliable as Turner Kennedy, to make that happen.

She was not letting Turner disrupt her carefully planned world!

CHAPTER FOUR

"ARE YOU HAPPY, Casey?" Turner asked softly.

The question was a disruption of her carefully planned world. And it was what she least expected. Not suave. Not teasing. Not flirtatious. She hated that he had asked that, because even if she didn't answer him—and she certainly did not intend to— she had to answer it to herself.

She had to get her guard back up!

"Of course I'm happy," she said, in a tone with so much bite she sounded anything but.

Happy? She was suddenly and achingly aware she was the furthest thing from happy. She was a woman who had experienced way too many losses in much too quick a succession.

Was it fair to have a baby to make herself happy?

Ridiculous to ask herself that! The point would be to make the baby happy. To give it the joyous, stable, wonderful family she had always craved.

Her life would finally be on track. She would have someone to live for, and to love!

This was just what he had done that night of Cole and Emily's wedding. Sitting with Casey on a darkened stretch of grass under a star-studded sky, wrapped in a blanket, Turner Kennedy had pulled her secret longings from her one by one, leaving her vulnerable and exposed.

Making her do something crazy. *Run away with me. Just pretend I'm a prince....*

And then, she reminded herself, leaving her. Period.

"And I'll be even happier when you hand over my keys," she said.

The keys dropped into her hand with a cold jingle. "I liked your hair better the way it was before."

"Thank you. You said that already. I'll take your opinion under careful consideration."

"You do that."

That was better. A certain awkwardness between them, as if they had never shared anything at all.

And then it all changed in a split second.

Bang.

The noise, a huge boom above their heads, was deafening in the quiet night. Before she knew what had happened, she was on the floor of the porch, Turner's hard body on top of her, shielding her, crushing the breath out of her.

A logical mind, which Casey's usually was, would have screamed *Danger!*

And she felt danger, all right, but not the kind that came from some unknown threat on the roof!

Silence settled again, and then was broken by the hiss of something sliding through the snow across the roof.

Turner's arms tightened around Casey, even as he peered upward. And while he was totally focused on the dangers above them, she was totally focused on the danger within her.

Casey could feel an intense sensation of heightened awareness. She could feel the crush of his chest against her breast, could count the ridges of his ribs where they were pressed into hers.

She could feel the coiled tension in arm muscles folded around her, and where the hard line of his thigh met the softer line of hers. She could feel the steady, elevated tattoo of his heart and the ragged beat of her own.

He was so close she could see the shadow of whiskers darkening the exquisite cut of his cheekbones, his jaw. She could see the perfect texture of his skin.

His scent—pine trees and cool mountain lakes—enveloped her.

Her scientific mind insisted on posing a question: Why was it that she felt so safe, when it was obvious he felt anything but?

She stared up into his face and knew, suddenly,

that it had worked both ways during those long-ago few days.

Turner Kennedy had seen her as no one else ever had. But she had seen him, too, felt she had known things about him. Now, studying his face as he squinted up toward the porch ceiling, she put her finger on what was different about him.

During those playful days, Turner Kennedy had seemed hopeful and filled with confidence. He had told her about losing his dad under very hard circumstances, but she had been struck by a certain faith in himself to change all that was bad about the world.

Now, Casey was aware she was looking into the face of a warrior—calm, strong, watchful. Ready.

And also, deeply weary. There was a hard-edged cynicism about him that went deeper than cynical. It went to his soul.

Casey knew that just as she had known things about him all those years ago. It was as if, with him, she arrived at a different level of knowing with almost terrifying swiftness.

And the other thing she knew?

Turner Kennedy was ready to protect her with his life.

A second passed and then two, but they were long, drawn-out seconds, as if time had come to an amazing standstill.

This was what chemicals did, she told herself

dreamily. He thought, apparently, they were in mortal danger.

She was bathing in the intoxicating closeness of him.

Casey could feel the strong beat of his heart through the thin fabric of his shirt. He was radiating a silky, sensual warmth, and she could feel the exact moment that his muscles began to uncoil. She observed the watchfulness drain from his expression, felt the thud of his heart quieting.

Finally, he looked away from the roof and gazed intently down at her.

Now that his mind had sounded some kind of all-clear, he, too, seemed to be feeling the pure chemistry of their closeness. His breath caressed her face like the touch of a summer breeze. She could feel her own heart picking up tempo as his began to slow. His mouth dropped closer to hers.

The new her, the one that was going to be impervious to the chemistry of pure attraction, seemed to be sitting passively in the backseat instead of the driver's seat. Because instead of giving Turner a much deserved shove—fight—or scooting out from under him—flight—she licked her lips, and watched his eyes darken and his lips drop even closer to hers.

But then the dog whined, did her best to insert her furry self between them, and licked Casey's face.

"Ugh!" She spat in pure disappointment. A dog's kiss instead of his!

But at least it had brought Casey to her senses. She managed to get her hands up in between them, and pushed.

Turner reared back off her, got his legs under him, leaped up with ease. But when she went to rise, too, he glanced at her, his expression once again remote. Stern, even. She didn't question her obedience when he held up his hand, stilling her while he scanned the darkness.

He went and leaned out over the porch railing, glanced up, and she could see whatever tension that remained in him dissipate completely.

He turned back to her, looking faintly sheepish. When he stretched out his hand to her, she took it, felt the chemical reaction again to his touch, his easy strength as he pulled her to her feet. He made an awkward attempt to brush off her jacket, then gave up.

"Sorry," he said. "I overreacted."

She thought of his lips nearly claiming hers, but apparently that wasn't what he felt he had overreacted to.

"A branch from this oak tree broke under the weight of the snow and landed on the roof."

She glanced where he was looking, and saw a huge limb had broken off, hit the porch roof and slid down it. Part of the broken branch was visible where it hung off the edge.

"What did you think it was?" she asked him softly.

He shrugged. "Who knows?"

Something made her push, but she wasn't sure what. Certainly it wasn't the self-preservation of fight or flight. "What did you think it was?" she asked again.

This time he rolled his shoulders, looked away, then back at her, obviously pained by her persistence.

"What?"

"I thought it was an explosion," he said quietly.

She took in again the expression on his face, registered the warrior way that he carried himself and had reacted.

"Where have you been, Turner?" she murmured. "Where have you been that your first thought would be it was an explosion?"

He looked away, gazed out into the darkness of the night. When he turned back, a small smile toyed with the edges of his mouth. But she could see it hid more than it revealed, and that was the way he wanted it.

"Why?" he asked. "Were you waiting for a postcard?"

Something dangerously close to sympathy for

him had been rising in her. Now, his sardonic tone erased that.

As if her hair loved all the fuss it was causing tonight, a strand, loosened from gel hell by the humidity of the wetly falling snow, sprang free and curled wildly. She blew it out of her eyes. "You know, it wouldn't take much for you to succeed at making me angry."

"Now, *that* is something I would really like to see," he said, unperturbed. "Though if knocking you to the floor didn't do it, I'm probably safe from your temper for tonight."

"Don't be so sure. Maybe I wasn't expecting a postcard, but would it have been so hard? To wake me up before you left that morning? To call just once to let me know what you were doing? To write a little note saying you enjoyed the days we spent together? To let me know you were all right?"

He didn't say anything, just looked at her steadily. She ordered herself to shut up, but she didn't.

"Nothing," she said, hoping it was anger and not pain he heard. "Not a single, solitary word. I'm surprised you even remembered my name, let alone my hair. And my brother. And my brother's name. And the way I feel at Christmas."

"I've never forgotten anything about you."

Some horrible weakness uncurled within her, but she saw it as completely forgivable since her defenses had been weakened by being pinned under him on the floor.

"That surprises me," she said coolly. She ordered herself to leave it there, but then reconsidered. They were going to be spending time here under the same roof, working toward the same goal of creating a perfect day for Emily and Cole.

Maybe there were some things they needed to get out of the way, that should be addressed so the tension between them didn't spoil things for others.

"I thought I would hear from you again," she said.

"I made it clear from the outset. I had three days. *We* had three days. That was all."

But she had thought those three days would change everything. She had nursed the hope that whatever mysterious thing was taking him away, the pull of what existed between them would prove irresistible! She had thought she would be able to wheedle his secret out of him, but she hadn't been able to, and in truth, hadn't that been part of the excitement? His mystery?

"Yes, you made that abundantly clear," she said coolly. "But you never said why."

"It's a long time ago," he said wearily.

"You're the one who brought up the postcard you never sent."

He sighed.

She could feel color rising in her cheeks. The last

thing she would ever want him to know was how she had waited. And believed. That he would call. That he would come back. That he had felt it, too.

An intensity of connection that had left her bereft as she had accepted he wasn't going to call. He wasn't coming back.

"It didn't have anything to do with you," he said, as if he could see suddenly in her eyes, despite the fact she was trying to guard her thoughts from him, all those desperate nights of waiting for him. The unexpected gentleness in his tone nearly undid her.

He raised his hand, as if to touch her throat or her hair again, but she stepped back. She was not sure what she would do if he touched her.

What she would want to do, that crazy gypsy dancer inside her, drenched in the chemical reaction to having his body over hers moments ago, would be to turn her head and catch his fingertips with her lips.

So she pulled her coat tighter around her, dropped her keys in one of the deep side pockets, and let her hand follow them. Suddenly, she realized how easily he had deflected her when she had asked him where he was. He had turned the question, making it about her instead. Was it possible he had even irritated her on purpose?

"You never did say where you went, why you had only three days." Did she sound as if she was begging for an explanation? She hated that! She had begged for an explanation then, to no avail.

At the time she had taken his "let's just live for the moment" as a sign of how wonderful everything was, not a warning that there would be only those moments.

He hesitated, looked away from her and then looked back, frowning.

"That night of Em and Cole's wedding, those crazy days in New York with you, that was the last time I was in *that* world. I left it behind completely," he admitted softly. "I left it behind completely because that is what I had trained to do. Immerse myself in a new reality. If I even glanced back, I would not have been able to perform."

"Emily thought you were in France! Or Italy."

He snorted.

"Perform what?" Casey whispered.

But he looked closed now, even annoyed with himself, and equally annoyed with her, as if she had dragged state secrets out of him.

And suddenly she wondered how close that was to the truth. A shadowy job no one seemed to know that much about, even his closest friends. A contractor for the government. And now, reacting to a snapping branch as if a gun had gone off. Or an explosion.

She absorbed it, along with the new air about him. "You're a spy," she guessed.

But his expression was closed now, completely unforthcoming.

"Bond," he said drily. "James Bond."

It was sarcastic, and it was a deflection. But it was not a denial.

"Are you?"

"A spy?" he said, and laughed, but it was a sound without humor. "That would imply a certain level of glamor, and I'm afraid nothing could be further from the truth. I've held some contracts that were sensitive."

"Secret?" she guessed.

He shrugged, shutting her out. His glance warned her *no more*.

And he was right. She was being way too interested.

Sucked in was more like it. Turner Kennedy's substantial charm was now layered with something dark and dangerous. Plus there was that chemical-inducing moment of lying beneath him….

Turner shook a cigarette from the pack in his pocket, stuck it in the corner of his mouth and spoke around it. "What are you doing wandering around out here, lingerie-filled suitcase in hand, in the middle of the night, anyway?"

She was tempted to protest that her suitcase was not *filled* with lingerie.

But then she saw it for what it was. Turner was moving the subject, again, away from himself.

She certainly was not going to admit she was escaping him!

"What are *you* doing out here at this time of night?" she asked him.

"I don't sleep well."

It was time for her to go. Really. She had her keys. Her dignity was intact. Why feel sympathetic that he didn't sleep?

But she had something to prove, too. That she could stand out here and talk to him and be completely unaffected by it, even if he had nearly crushed her body under his, even if the dog had stolen his kiss from her lips.

"I don't remember you smoking."

He laughed. "I don't. Not anymore." He took the cigarette, glared at it for a moment, then tossed it over the railing. "But when I can't sleep, I wish I did."

She knew again that there was a dark place in Turner Kennedy that had not been there before.

Casey fought a desire to lighten it somehow—she wasn't sure how. Tell a joke, give a hug, something purely feminine and nurturing. Biology joining with chemistry to make a knockout punch for those who were not careful.

But she was nothing if not careful. Nothing about this encounter was in her script for her completely fulfilling life of solitude and simple pleasures like yoga and calligraphy.

"Smoking is very bad for you," she said primly.

"Thanks, Doc," he said, "I'll take that under consideration."

Something about his voice made her think that whatever he had been doing, smoking paled as a danger.

And something about the way he held himself told her other truths. He felt as alone as she did. And maybe not just at Christmas, either.

"Why are you here for Christmas?" he asked suddenly, abruptly, as if he was irritated that she had decided to come. "You have family."

"There's just my mom. She had, er, other plans."

Something like sympathy crossed the rugged barrier of his closed face, and Casey rushed on. "It's not a big deal. I feel my connection with Emily and Andrea is as strong as a family bond. Besides, don't you think this will be a lovely place to spend Christmas? Almost like a fairy tale."

"Do I look like I believe in fairy tales?" His voice sounded harsh, not that of a man who had once said, "Just pretend I'm a prince...."

"No, you don't," she said. She would like to add she didn't, either, but she still did, to a certain extent. No prince, but Casey wanted to create fairy-tale Christmases for her child.

Weaknesses she should be happy to unearth!

"How hokey do you think it's going to be?" he asked.

"Terribly."

"Christmas-carols-around-the-fire hokey?"

"Definitely."

"Hell."

"Tut-tut, that's not exactly in the spirit of the season."

He smiled reluctantly.

"What were you expecting from a place called the Gingerbread Inn, gladiator games?"

"Touché," he said drily.

"You have a family, too," she remembered. In the days together he had revealed that much of himself. His was as different from hers as night was from day, except that both families had experienced tragedy. Her brother, when she was young; his father in the World Trade Center attacks.

Hadn't that been part of what had drawn her to him, moth to flame? That Turner knew what it was to be part of a normal family? By his descriptions, the Kennedys had been fun-loving, wholesome, all-American.

What kind of weakness was it that she could remember every single word he had said to her?

"I thought your family did hokey," she said thoughtfully. "One year you told me you got a puppy for Christmas, for goodness sake!"

A subtle line of strain appeared around his mouth. "My mom died while I was overseas."

"I'm so sorry. But your brothers? You had two of

them, right? Younger than you?" She smiled. "The backyard skating rink."

Something in his face closed. "Things change."

Her need for self-preservation dissolved, and this time it was Casey who reached out. She placed her fingers on his wrist, then closed them around it. "*That* changes?"

Despite her resolve to place her belief in different things, she felt shocked. A close family, one as close as he had described, could become estranged? By what?

"Everything changes," he said, and his voice was weary and cynical. "That's the only thing you can count on. That everything can change. And it does. You should go inside now."

He slipped his wrist free of her grasp, but she couldn't move. She told herself it was because she was not allowing him to tell her what to do, but she knew that wasn't really it. Not even close.

"You should go inside," he said softly, "before I do something I'd regret even more than lighting that cigarette."

She didn't have to ask him what.

His eyes lingered on her lips and a memory sizzled in the air between them. She felt a disgusting weakness.

A desire to lean toward him and take his lips, and then pull back and say, "Regret, hmm?"

But instead, she pretended she didn't have a clue

what he was talking about, pretended she was immune to the pull between them.

She cocked her head. "What would that be?"

CHAPTER FIVE

THE SMILE WAS back. The one that guarded what Turner Kennedy was thinking. He dragged his eyes slowly, and without a bit of apology, away from her lips. "I was going to go shovel off a piece of the lake and go skating."

She saw now that as well as the adoring dog, he had skates at his feet.

"It's three o'clock in the morning!"

"I told you. Can't sleep. That's why I'd regret it if I asked you to come with me. Night can make strange things happen between people. Things that normally wouldn't. Or maybe shouldn't."

He was talking about that night all those years ago when he had impulsively invited her to run away with him. When he had warned her there would be a time limit, and she had allowed herself not to believe it.

"You probably haven't been up at three in the morning since then," he said huskily, and she hated that he could read her mind.

So she said, raising an eyebrow, "Since when?"

Turner just chuckled, not fooled.

She turned and walked away from him, her steps deliberate and unhurried. She picked up her suitcase from where she had dropped it by the door. The screen squealed when she opened it, but it wasn't loud enough to cover the soft sound of his mocking laughter that he'd been right.

That despite the red lace, the only thing wild about her was her hair.

And if the pounding in her heart and the flame in her cheeks were any indication, she was just as susceptible to him.

The next day, she felt so tired. She had fallen asleep, finally, near dawn to the sound of Turner's shovel scraping the ice.

She noticed he looked exhausted, too, as all the friends came together for a simple breakfast of cereal, and to make a plan for the day.

Andrea had made an extensive list of jobs, large and small, that needed to be accomplished, and Casey was relieved that Turner's enthusiasm for the ice had been noted, and he had been put in charge of getting the lake ready for a skating party after the vow renewal ceremony was over on Christmas Eve.

He either took it very seriously or had no desire to be with the rest of them. All day she could hear him shoveling an ever widening space to skate. It seemed as if he would not be satisfied until the whole lake was cleared.

Casey, assigned inside decorating jobs, would go peer out the window and watch him guiltily when it seemed no one would notice,

Watching a strong man tackle all that snow with easy grace and confidence was a shockingly beautiful sight. The lake ice began to emerge from under the blanket of yesterday's snowfall, and it shone, bright as gunmetal.

Sometimes he seemed to grow bored with shoveling. Then he would turn his attention to making a fire pit and building rough benches. He looked as wonderful splitting wood as he did shoveling snow.

He did not come in for lunch or supper. When Emily wanted to go get him, as they all sat around the hearth in the parlor going over the day, eating Carol's amazing apple pie and visiting, Cole just shook his head.

"Leave him be," he said, something troubled in his eyes when he thought of his friend.

Casey went to bed without seeing him, annoyed with herself that she could feel Turner Kennedy's presence at the inn, and a faint agitation that went with it, without even having any face-to-face contact with him.

She woke to pitch blackness, not sure what had woken her, but drawn to the window. Her bedroom was on the back side of the house, facing the lake, and Casey flicked back a heavy curtain that had left the pane frosted, while not keeping out the draft.

Her eyes adjusted to the inky darkness. She was shocked to see Turner was still down at the lake. He sat on one of his benches, but hadn't lit a fire. He had on that ultrasexy parka with a fur-lined hood. The shovel was propped against the bench and he seemed to be contemplating the rink he'd made.

Then he got up, and she saw he had skates on. He made his way gracefully from the snow-covered bank to the ice.

And he began to skate.

If she had thought watching him pit his power against snow clearing and splitting wood was a wonder, it was nothing compared to this.

Turner was extraordinary on skates. He raced over the ice with effortless grace, his incredible power and energy practically shimmering in the cold air around him.

Harper was skittering along after Turner, joyous at this unusual nocturnal excursion.

Stop watching, Casey told herself. But she couldn't.

All those years ago, with him, she had felt magic. She was not sure she had ever felt it since. He was right; people did not make good decisions in the middle of the night. Because she suddenly wanted to skate.

"I should go skating," she whispered, watching him.

Such an irrational thought shook the scientist in her to her core. It was the middle of the night. She wasn't a great skater. She had not once in her whole life felt compelled to go skating.

She thought of the way Turner's gaze had locked on her lips when he had talked about doing something he would regret. She knew she was playing with fire.

Then, as she watched, Turner stopped for a moment, leaned over and grabbed some snow from the edge of the rink he had cleared. With his bare hands he formed it into a ball, then threw it for the eagerly waiting dog.

Harper scrambled after it, burrowed beneath the snow looking for it, came back to him empty-jawed, with a bewildered shake of her golden head, begging him to throw another, whining that she would do better next time.

He should have laughed. It was funny.

But he didn't. One thing Casey remembered from that night they had spent together was the easiness of his laughter, the goldenness of it, as if it had the power to chase away shadows.

The dog rolled over in front of him, her legs in the air. Still, he did not laugh at her attempt to charm him. He gave her belly a quick pat and went back to work.

Casey knew this was the time to let the curtain

fall back into place, and climb back under the cozy, worn feather duvet on her bed.

"After all," she muttered, "he didn't even ask you. In fact, he made a point of *not* asking you."

He was making a point of being by himself.

If ever there was a time in her life to be safe and rational and totally true to her predictable nature, this was it. She finally had a plan for herself. For her future, and her contentment!

She had passed the first test, the first encounter with Turner. She had passed it despite the fact that she remembered too much, and despite the fact she'd been crushed under his body and, shamefully, had loved it.

She had passed again today, leaving him alone, not seeking him out. Not, she hoped, giving anyone the slightest indication that she had been tense all day at the thought of him joining them, and then oddly disappointed when he hadn't.

So she had passed. She didn't think anyone had guessed that Turner created turmoil in her. That being under the same roof as him felt like a form of torture. Their past history made her feel angry at him. And embarrassed for herself. But that wasn't all she felt. She wished it was. No, she felt confused by him, and by her reactions to him.

So she let the curtain fall, made herself go back to bed, and ordered herself to sleep. But the scien-

tist in her did not like confusion. The scientist demanded a solution.

If she didn't go out there, was she damned to
this state of confusion? Had he won in some way?
Intimidated her? He was probably even now congratulating himself on how correct his assessment
of her had been, despite underwear that screamed
the opposite.

That the only thing wild about Casey Caravetta
was her hair.

Lying here in bed was the flight option.

It was what he expected of her. And what she expected of herself. And in all honesty, where had that
got her, so far? Is this what she wanted to teach her
future child? To hide from life and its challenges?

No! She wanted to go into motherhood confident
of her ability to be in control of herself at all times,
so her children would never know the insecurities
of a childhood buffeted by the passions and weaknesses of the adults around them. Casey could not
run from challenges. She had to accept them! And
conquer them!

Feeling not like someone who had said yes to
fun, but like an ancient woman warrior girding herself for battle, she went to her suitcase and found a
warm pair of slacks and a wool sweater.

She shoved every single strand of her wildly
curling hair under a simple black toque.

***

Turner had never lost his love of skating. The ice and the work and the solitude he was finding at the inn were a balm to his tumultuous soul.

The lake ice reminded him of his father's backyard rinks—imperfect and lumpy, not like the perfectly made ice in skating rinks at all.

The memory of his father—wanting to honor his father—had driven every major decision of his life since 2001.

So how had it all turned out so differently from what he would have wanted? And certainly differently from what his father would have wanted for him.

Turner remembered only good things from his childhood. Racing his brothers in tight loops around the backyard rink, roughhousing, spending summers haunting the nearby beaches.

He had grown up in one of those wealthy satellite communities, less than a half hour commute to New York City. His family had been fun-loving, traditional and well-to-do. He had never aspired to anything except to follow in his father's footsteps. Turner had had every expectation he would marry, have a wonderful home, re-create for his own children the idyllic childhood he'd had.

He had been in his first year of university when the World Trade Center had been attacked. At 9:59 a.m. on September 11, 2001, the South Tower, where his father worked as a financial manager, collapsed.

The Kennedy family had collapsed at the same time.

Within months, Turner had made a decision to leave university and join the military. He'd felt as if everything his father had stood for was threatened, and he had felt he could not stand by and not try to change a world gone terribly wrong.

In very short order, Turner had been singled out and selected for membership in Tango, an elite and highly classified antiterrorism unit. The cover story was that he handled sensitive "contracts" for the government.

As he had said to Casey, those days with her had been his last in the world he'd known.

He was amazed by how his first discussion with her had been so fraught with the topic of miracles—and that he had started it!

Because he had been in a position many times where he had pleaded for one. And not been on the receiving end. The last time, just a few months ago. It had been an extremely dangerous assignment. The odds had been against them from the start. A far better man than he—Ken Hamilton, a man who had needed to live, for his wife and his family—had died in Turner's arms.

When Turner was young—and hopelessly naive—he had embraced a dangerous way of life, thinking it would give him a sense of meaning, a sense of bringing order to a chaotic world.

Instead, with Ham's death, it had felt as if something broke in him. If he had had even a sliver of faith left, it was gone now. Turner Kennedy was a man who had lost the sense that anything had meaning. Life was random. And unpredictable.

When it was out of your control, you were in trouble. Period.

Now, as he skated, with the dog chasing him joyously, he knew why he had come here. It was different from the reason he had thought.

He had told himself it was to try and get a good night's sleep. It felt like months since he had slept, not been awakened by dreams, soaked in sweat. He always feared he was soaked in the stickiness of blood, until he turned on a light.

He told himself you didn't let down a buddy who asked. And Cole had asked, said he *needed* him to help get this falling-down old inn ready for a special day, the most important day of his life.

"I have an opportunity to make my world right again," Cole had said. "I've been given a second chance. I want the day to be as perfect as it can be for Emily. Will you come be part of it? Will you come help me?"

The possibility that there was such a thing as a second chance had lured Turner here.

He had come to help a friend. That was as engrained in him now as breathing. You helped your buddies when they asked.

But he knew he'd come to help himself, too.

To see if there was any chance at all for normalcy for him. A normal night's sleep. A normal life.

A long time ago he had stood at a crossroad and had taken a turn. The choice had cost him more than he had ever expected to pay.

Could a man backtrack to the same crossroad and choose differently? Could he, who had seen and done so many things that were outside the experience of the average American—certainly outside that of his brothers, who were raising their own families now—could he bring anything back to them except pure poison? A cold, hard heart? A damaged spirit?

What good could that do anyone?

No, maybe his other option was the right one. Sign up again. And again. And again. Until he joined his other brothers, the ones who had shared those experiences. Until all of them lay beneath the ground, where they could be mourned as heroes, without forcing their families to tolerate them as they were: damaged, cynical, unable to connect with the ordinary things that ordinary people thought were fun and exciting.

That's why he had come to the Gingerbread Inn. To see if there really were second chances. And to make a choice.

Out of the corner of his eye, he caught movement. Through the darkness, in a pink snowsuit that looked almost neon against the white snow, Casey was coming toward the lake.

Now there was a woman who was going to complicate a simple choice.

There was a woman who could shake his sense of control. And that meant trouble. Period.

And yet all those years ago, when he had spent that time in New York with her, he had done it with the purest of motivations. Yes, he'd been intent on making his final days in the States fun and carefree. Maybe he had known, at some level, he was leaving a world behind forever.

But it had been more than evident to him that while he had grown up in a fun and carefree environment—with backyard skating rinks and puppies delivered by Santa—that was a side of life she had never, because of her brother's illness, completely known. Casey had never been carefree.

He had just wanted to show her something. What life could be like.

That moment when Casey, drowning in the Waldorf Astoria housecoat, had given in completely, taken his hand and jumped up and down with him on the king-size bed in the master bedroom of the suite, laughing out loud, he'd felt he had succeeded at something.

Setting the rather uptight Miss Caravetta free. In

that moment, the truth he thought he had glimpsed about her had proved to be wonderfully true.

But it seemed she had gone backward since then. He hadn't been in the inn much, but Casey seemed more uptight than ever, as if she had rebounded back to where she had been before, and then some.

Because of him? Because he had left her without saying goodbye? Certainly that couldn't be all of it. And just as certainly, it couldn't have helped.

After those three days, he'd had a sense of knowing her, through and through. How sweetly sensitive she was, how deep, how serious. He had known there would be tears if they had a formal farewell.

His fear of tears was not a new one, like his fear of sleeping, and the fear of Christmas that was keeping him out on this lake while everyone else was busy getting ready. By the time he had met Casey that first time, he had had enough tears to last him a lifetime. And so he had just slipped out the door that morning.

So why did he feel faintly but unmistakably happy to see her coming, when it was the last thing he'd expected of her, and when he was a man who did not like to be surprised by life?

Because it meant something of that girl who had jumped on the bed remained.

It meant maybe he had been given a second chance to do the right thing. It meant maybe he could get to see her laugh again.

That part of it had elements of selfishness in it. But a memory of a laugh like hers could hold a man in the light when his life took him to dark places.

This would be the challenge. To bring her back to that place of carefree laughter, without ever letting her see that he could not truly go there with her. Not anymore.

Even back then, maybe he had hoped carefree joy was a baton he was passing to her. The training, though not real, had foreshadowed the real thing. Even before actually going on that first mission, a baptism in blood and fire, Turner had probably known that particular baton—joyous abandon—would not be his to hold again.

She had every inch of her hair tucked up under a toque, and for some reason, her not wanting to give him even a glimpse of those locks that he had confessed to adore made him smile. Getting her to let her hair back down was going to be a challenge.

It felt like the first truly genuine smile he'd had in months.

As she approached the lake, Casey watched Turner skate with a sense of awe. She had not been around people who were athletic, and certainly outdoor sports of any kind were not part of her rather bookish experience.

She paused and looked at him.

He wasn't skating, he was flying. Bent slightly

at the waist, legs crossing over each other in the turns, seamlessly moving from skating forward to skating backward.

There was incredible energy in the air around him. This was his confidence and his strength showing in a very outward way.

His proficiency rattled her! She had never even been on skates. She was sure she was about to make a fool of herself, and almost headed back, except that suddenly he threw his weight to one side, and in a spray of scraped ice, came to a halt.

He had seen her. If she retreated now, she had lost more surely than if she had not come down here in the first place.

There was a bench beside the lake and Casey stopped at it to put on the skates she had chosen from the vast array hung on pegs inside the inn's back door, for the use of guests.

While she glared down at the skates, suddenly his dark hair appeared in her peripheral vision.

She braced herself for him to ask why she was here, what she wanted from him, but he didn't. His dark head bent over her skates. She had to bite her lip to fight the urge to touch it. This was so much like the night he had playfully painted her toenails.

"Red," he'd said, "hidden inside your shoes, like a secret between us."

His hands were on the laces. "Nice and tight," he said. "They're terrible skates. I'll see if the laces are long enough to wrap around your ankles for more support."

She glared at his head. He could at least act surprised that she had come! But then again, she had the feeling he had become a man it would take a great deal to surprise. And a woman wanting to spend time with him would not be one of those things!

"Okay." He gave her skates a little slap. "I think you're ready."

She was not sure what she had pictured, but possibly gliding around him with swanlike elegance had been part of her it.

Too late, Casey realized some skating experience would undoubtedly have helped in creating such a picture.

She waddled from the bench to the ice with about as much grace as a penguin making its annual march.

She was sure once she actually got to the lake, like a penguin making it to water, all that would change, and his next words made her think it would, too.

"Do you believe in miracles, Casey?" he asked softly.

"No," she said, astonished at the quaver in her voice. "Of course not! I'm a scientist."

He regarded her thoughtfully, a faint cynical upturn to his mouth. "I don't believe in them, either," he said softly. "But I wish you did."

"Why?"

He rolled his shoulders. He was obviously exhausted. She was not sure he had slept since he'd arrived here.

"If you give up believing in miracles," he told her quietly, "then you believe only in yourself. And then when you fail there is nothing left to believe in."

She stood there, frozen to the spot, knowing he had just trusted her with something of himself, and the regret he felt was already etched in his face.

He covered it quickly. "So here, Casey, let me give you a miracle."

He held out his hand to her, and tentatively, she took it. And it did feel as if a miracle shivered to life within her.

Everything that had hurt her about love seemed to disintegrate. *Oh, no.* This was the opposite of what she had come here to prove! She should have refused his hand. She should have insisted on doing this herself!

But Turner Kennedy had her now, and he pulled her forward, off the snowy bank and onto the ice.

One foot slid annoyingly away as she tried to anchor the other on the slippery surface. He let go of her hand and she stood there, frozen to the spot.

He was skating backward, as if it was as easy

for him as breathing, and watching her. When her leg skittered even farther away, he skated back toward her with a breathtaking burst of speed, leaped forward, took her elbow.

"I'll give you a hand."

It would be churlish to refuse, not to mention there was a very real possibility that without him steadying her she was going to fall flat on her fanny without having skated a single step.

He placed one hand around her shoulder and the other at her waist, and persuaded her to allow her other foot to be guided to the ice.

Even leaning heavily against him, Casey was wobbling. "I feel like an elephant trying to balance on a beach ball," she said.

"What? You don't get the miracle?"

"Miracle?" She was very aware, for the second time since their reunion, that they were touching physically.

And for the second time, she felt as if she could count on him. Lean on him. That he would protect her with his life, if need be.

That was a miracle even if it was quite a lot to read into the fact that he was holding her up so she wouldn't hit the ice with a very painful splat.

"It's a miracle of biblical proportions," he whispered huskily in her ear. "You're walking on water."

Despite herself, she laughed. And then he smiled, and it was a real smile, even lightening the exhaustion around his eyes. He steadied her on her feet. "You've never skated, have you?"

"That's why I'm here," she said mutinously. "I'm all about embracing life's adventures."

He snorted, but gently. "Since when?"

"Hey, I'm the girl who ran away with you once."

"So you are," he said quietly.

"It was the most impulsive thing I had ever done. I lied to my parents about where I was."

"I know."

"I mean, I shouldn't have had to lie to them. I was old enough to do what I wanted."

"Nothing happened that you couldn't tell your parents about."

"That's true. It didn't really work out for me. Embracing adventure. But here I am again. Wouldn't you say that was brave?"

He said nothing.

"Or stupid," she said, as if she had read his thoughts. "You know what the difference is this time?"

He shook his head.

"Me," she said. "I'm different from how I was back then."

He looked relieved and as if he didn't believe her at the very same time.

"I am," she insisted.

"I didn't say anything."

"It was years ago."

"I didn't say anything."

"I'm not needy."

"Okay."

"It just looked like fun. To come out here and skate. No strings attached. Put the past behind us. I don't have a crush on you. That's what I'm saying. That girl is gone."

"Okay," he repeated quietly.

"So, if we've got that straightened away, let's go."

"Let's," he said, and even though he had agreed with every single thing she had said, she was not sure he had believed a word that had come out of her mouth.

And worse…she was not sure that she had, either!

"Someday," she said with grim determination, "I want to teach my children how to skate. That's really why I'm here."

CHAPTER SIX

"I'M GLAD YOU cleared that up," Turner said solemnly, "Now hold on."

He moved the hand around her waist to her wrist. In a blink, he had pulled away, spun around and was facing her.

He took both her hands firmly in his. He had gloves on, she had mittens, but she could still feel a surge of energy pouring between them. He moved effortlessly backward, pulling her toward him.

"Don't look at your feet," he said.

"What am I supposed to look at?"

"Me."

That's what she was afraid of. Because looking into his crystal clear gray eyes made it too easy to forget she was on a mission. That she was here to start laying the groundwork for her child's—or children's—future. She was here to prove something.

To him.

Most especially to herself.

But that mission was feeling like a mirage in a desert. The closer she got to him, the more it seemed to disappear.

"That's it," he said approvingly. "Hey, look, you're skating."

She wasn't really, and she knew it. She was wobbling after him like a baby frantic not to lose sight of its mother.

"Now," he said, "as miraculous as it is to walk on water, I want you to quit trying to walk. Skating is all about gliding. So push off with your right foot, and let your left one slide forward. Hey! That was good."

The mission dissolved a little more as she got caught up in the motion. Push. Glide. Push. Glide. Right foot, then left one.

"Let go of my hands."

Embarrassingly, he had to pry her hands from his.

"Keep looking at me. Hey! No looking at your feet."

He moved away from her, and she scrambled after him like a clumsy puppy. He smiled. That smile was a carrot worth racing toward!

Wait! It wasn't. Her whole future felt as if it could be decided in these moments. She was not leaning! She was not depending. She was doing it all herself, her way. She was getting the hang of this thing. She didn't need Turner Kennedy or anyone, and in the interest of making that point, she turned from him and skated off in another direction.

She made it a few yards before one foot decided to go one way and one the other, and her arms windmilled in a crazy attempt to stop herself from falling, but—

Splat.

"Ouch," she said, "That hurt!" Her pride as much as her derriere!

He skated over and held out his hands. She saw he was smiling that genuine smile again. Why did she feel it had become so rare?

She saw no option but to take his hands, and he hauled her up with easy strength. Strength it would be far too easy to rely on! Casey swatted his hands away as soon as she was standing. He raised his palms in mock surrender.

She skated this way and that, experimenting, falling, getting back up. He gave her instructions, called suggestions, came and grabbed her elbow when she was going to fall over. Together, they covered every inch of the ice that he had shoveled off.

She realized she may have started out to prove something, but she was having fun! Suddenly, she realized she shouldn't be having fun. She shouldn't be letting her guard down.

In truth, he was setting up the very same dynamic he had that evening of the wedding.

He was the suave and sophisticated slightly older

man; she was the gauche girl bowled over by his attention.

He was taking the lead. He was going to decide what happened and when.

Including, like that other time, making a decision never to see her again!

Well, this time it wasn't going to be like that. She was not going to play little sister to his big brother. She had surprised him by showing up on the ice, and she was going to continue to surprise him.

And herself.

She had something to prove! That she could resist his damnable attractions. And at the same time, prove that she was not his little sister, not even close.

Deliberately, she set off across the ice, away from him. She gained confidence. The sensation of flying was quite remarkable. It was fun and exciting to be moving across the frozen surface on her own, but the speed was surprising. Too soon, she reached the end of the shoveled part, and she had not learned anything about stopping yet!

She hit the snowbank at high speed and catapulted into it, facedown, rump in the air. She flipped over and spit snow out of her mouth, looking up at the inky, star-crusted sky.

"Argh." She tried to get up, but the skates made it nearly impossible to get her feet under her. She collapsed back into the snow.

Turner glanced over, then turned and raced toward her. "Are you okay?" He leaned down, held out his hands. She took them and let him yank her to her feet.

He pulled a little too hard and she fell against him, her feet wobbling.

She looked up at him, saw the soft clouds of warm breath leaving his mouth, his eyes lustrous as polished silver in the darkness.

No matter what she had told herself, she knew this was why she was really here. To feel this once again, if only ever so briefly. Uninhibited. Unfettered. Brave, somehow, as if life was an adventure she was willing to embrace.

Without any forethought, she reached up and touched her lips to his. He tasted of ice and magic, of moonlit nights and the sharp cut of skate blades. He tasted of the memory of carefree laughter, and a time when she had let go of all control.

She could feel that control slipping away again, blissfully, completely....

He pulled back from her, but couldn't let her go because she would fall again.

"Casey. What the hell are you doing?"

"Kissing you," she said huskily.

"That wasn't in the lesson plan."

Just as she had figured. He was teacher, she was student. As long as he was in control, everything was great.

"Get this straight," she said firmly, the magic of the kiss dissolving to embarrassment she didn't intend to let him see. "I am not your student. Or your little sister."

He let her go. Her ankles wobbled, but somehow she maintained her balance.

"Okay," he said, his arms folded over his chest, his voice remote. "I think we're clear on that."

And then he skated away from her, went to the edge of the ice, made the transition to the snow easily, and walked to the bench. He took off his skates without glancing at her, slung them over his shoulder, and with the dog's nose an inch from his thigh, headed for the inn.

What had she done? Casey wondered, watching him go. She'd given in to the temptation to be alive fully. But there was no excuse for using her lips to do it!

Besides, she had ended up not at all certain she could resist his appeal if she was put to the test. What had she expected?

That he was going to be helpless in the face of her charm. But why would he be? He hadn't been all those years ago, or he would have stayed, instead of left.

Still, she had a feeling she had just rattled Turner Kennedy, the unflappable, and she couldn't help but feel the smallest satisfaction over that.

Of course, she had rattled herself in the process.

Right to the core. She had never felt like that when she'd kissed Sebastian.

Oh, it had been pleasant enough.

When she had confronted Sebastian about his infidelity, he had said woefully that he'd never crossed "the line." He was so sorry. He was just testing the water, looking for something *more*.

When pressed, he hadn't been able to tell her what that "more" was, what it looked like or felt like, even though, presumably, he had been in hot pursuit of it with someone else.

But right now, Casey felt as if she knew exactly what *more* was. It was touching someone else and feeling the sizzle of his energy. It was tasting someone else, and feeling as if you were eating something you could never, ever get enough of. It was a longing, deep and primal, that suddenly felt as if only that one person could satisfy it.

That part Turner never had to know.

He had rejected her, which was sad only because she had planned to reject him first.

"For the sake of future generations," she told herself, as if it was a motto for battle.

She did a few more defiant if graceless spins around the ice, just to show him he could not affect her, that she was still having fun. But there were no witnesses to her lack of grace or her fun-filled effort.

Turner did not glance back.

Not even once.

* * *

Casey had kissed him! Hard not to give in to that, Turner thought. Hard not to explore the sweetness of her offered lips until Casey and he were both gasping with need and desire. Thankfully, she had arrived on the ice hard on the heels of his ruthless self-evaluation.

There was no sense him giving her the idea that he was the kind of guy she needed in her life. There was no sense in that at all.

He was not the kind of guy anyone needed in his or her life. That kiss, and the innocence in it, despite the fact she had intended to prove she was now a woman of the world, had led him one step closer to realizing he was too wounded to return to a place like her lips had offered him. Like his boyhood home. Like the homes of his brothers.

Not that anyone was rolling out the red carpet in welcome. His brothers had never felt he was vindicating the murder of their father. They had felt he had abandoned his family when he was most needed, that he had left his mother when she was at her most fragile.

His brothers saw him as going off to save the world when his own family was more in need of saving.

When he had not been able to come back for their mother's funeral, something had broken irrevocably between him and his brothers.

Casey should be careful whose lips she tangled with. With that in mind, Turner headed for the shower, hoping to wash the sweetness of her from his mind. He could not get rid of the dog. She pushed into the bathroom with him, waited in the steamy room until he was done.

An hour later, he hit the stairs at about the same time as another woman.

"Hi," she said, extending her hand. "Not sure why we haven't bumped into each other before. I'm Carol. I run the old place."

"Turner Kennedy."

Her hand was the hand of a woman who worked really, really hard, probably doing all kinds of things women weren't intended to do.

"Nice to meet you. And there's my missing dog! Harper, where have you been?"

"She was with me," Turner said.

"All night? Actually, for two nights?"

"Sorry if you worried. I tried to shake her, but she wasn't having any of it."

"How odd. I mean, she's a goldie, so she likes everyone, but I've never seen her become attached to anyone so completely before. Look, she's not leaving you even now."

Sure enough, after a token tail wag for her owner, the dog sat down beside him, leaning heavily into his leg.

"Poor judge of character," he said, but with a smile.

Carol regarded him with unwanted compassion. "I'd say the exact opposite is true, Mr. Kennedy. The dog knows exactly who you really are, even if you have lost sight of that yourself."

Turner was annoyed that his plan for long, mind-clearing days of hard work and skating had turned into something else—thanks to Casey. It now seemed his tormented soul was so close to the surface anyone who looked could see it.

"Nice meeting you," he said, eager to turn his back on Carol's way too perceptive gaze. He took the stairs two at a time and followed the smell of coffee into the kitchen.

"Hey," Carol said. "Harper, aren't you going to spend some time with me?"

But the dog cast her owner one faintly guilty look before wiggling through the swinging door with Turner just before it closed.

He heard Carol laugh tolerantly. He hoped to sneak into the kitchen and get a cup of coffee, and maybe *try* to sleep for a couple hours before seeing what Cole had planned for them today.

Maybe it hadn't been fair to these people to come here, either.

He'd seen that on Casey's face last night after he'd thought an IED had gone off, and he'd smacked her down to the floor. He might never be able to fit in.

Casey.

He had not succeeded in washing the sweetness of her kiss from his lips. Thinking of her made him ache for the road not taken.

In a way, Casey had been the beginning of his journey away from all he knew, and toward a job that forced him to make choices that hurt people, intentional or not.

Emily was in the kitchen. "Coffee's ready," she sang. "Oh, look, you've got a friend. Good morning, Harper."

The dog wagged her tail, but when Emily slapped her knee to coax her over, Harper sat down stubbornly on Turner's foot.

"I slipped her a doughnut," Turner lied, not wanting anyone making assumptions about the nature of his character just because the dog liked him.

He regarded Emily for a moment, and allowed himself to feel happy for the pure reason that his best friend's wife was happy, that maybe the Watsons were going to make it through the minefields that were relationships and life.

"The coffee smells good." Turner said, shaking the dog off his foot so he could get some.

"You're up early." She looked at him, "I bet you're going skating?"

"I've already been."

"This early?"

"Or late, depending how you look at it."

"Have you been up all night?"

"I have jet lag." It was the convenient lie he told to cover the fact he was having so much trouble sleeping.

"Where are you coming from? Oh, I remember. Cole said something about Turkey."

Turkey was not the exact location, of course. It wasn't even close; just a stop on the way to the end of the world. But he did not correct her.

"I remember you skating," Emily said, "from when Cole and I were dating. You were amazing. Weren't some hockey scouts interested in you?"

A road not taken. A carefree life of playing games. Turner never thought of that, because, inevitably, it would lead him to wonder who he might have been had he chosen a different fork in the road.

"That was a long time ago," he said, a little too harshly.

He rolled his shoulders. All these people, Emily and Cole, Andrea, Casey, despite the problems they might have suffered, still were what he was not.

They were basically good. Wholesome. Uncomplicated. Not one of them had ever had to make a decision about whether another human being got to live or die. Not one of them had ever sat with their best friend's blood soaking into their clothing.

Maybe he should not have come to a place where people were going to begin their sentences with the words *I remember*.

"Good coffee," Turner said, to move the subject away from his recent travels and the past.

"Thanks," Emily said. "It was an early Christmas gift. Melissa's folks sent it from Kona for Andrea and Casey and me. They retired there."

"Have you been to Hawaii?"

She took the bait easily, and Turner was relieved to hear her chatter about the beauty of the islands rather than the places where their histories had touched when she had first met Cole.

Casey came through the swinging kitchen doors, screeched to a halt when she saw him, then flounced by him to the coffeepot. "Good morning, Emily. Good morning, Harper."

No "Good morning, Turner." Well, she was a bright girl, probably the brightest he had ever met, a whole lot brighter than a golden retriever.

"Is this the coffee Melissa's parents sent? It's wonderful. That was so thoughtful of them." Casey took a sip and eyed him over the rim of her mug, while still not acknowledging him. "What can I help with?"

Turner noticed Casey had little smudges under her eyes from being up all night, but other than that she was an unconventional beauty. Her lips looked bruised. How could that be? They had shared about the shortest kiss in history!

She had showered before coming downstairs, and her hair, which looked as if it would take a day to dry completely, was curling as wildly as he ever remembered it. How could a man not dream of burying his hands in those wayward curls?

Had she left it like that because he had said he liked it that way?

She was not wearing a speck of makeup, her olive skin dewy from the shower, her eyes dark and deep. He looked at the puffy fullness of her lips again and knew it was going to be a long time before he shook off the taste of them, or the longing for it.

She had a beautiful figure, though she had lost some of the endearing chubbiness he remembered of her in her bridesmaid's dress. She still seemed to dress to understate, today in a buttoned-to-the-throat blouse that was too big for her, and a pair of jeans that looked as if she had tried to wrestle her curvy hips into a strait jacket.

"Well, I was thinking omelets," Emily said, a bit doubtfully. "Casey, if you want to start grating some cheese, that would be a big help. Do you remember Turner?"

Casey busied herself slamming through cabinets looking for a cheese grater, and she barely glanced at him.

"We bumped into each other," she said, her voice flat.

Literally, he thought, remembering her soft curves beneath his on the porch the other night, her clinging to him as he'd pulled her from the snow at the edge of the ice.

She managed to convey, without elaborating, that it had not been her favorite experience, which, of course, was repayment for the fact he had rejected her kiss.

For her own damn good.

But she had probably left her hair in that natural glorious state for his benefit, to torment him.

And damn, if it didn't seem to be working!

CHAPTER SEVEN

"I'LL JUST TAKE my coffee and leave you to it," Turner said.

He didn't miss the fact that Casey looked smug that she had managed to make him uncomfortable.

He was pretty sure she knew he was having trouble not watching her as she drew an elastic band from her slacks pocket and began to pull that wild hair back with elaborate care.

He wasn't sure why that was so sexy it was making his mouth go dry. Her hair didn't like being tamed, and little strands were already breaking out of the band, curling wildly.

"No you don't, Turner," Emily said with a laugh. "No chauvinism allowed. The little ladies are not going to fix you breakfast."

Casey snorted with satisfaction.

"I actually wasn't expecting breakfast," he said in his own defense.

"Well, I'm just learning to cook, believe it or not,

so I need all the help I can get. I'm regretting telling Carol I'd look after it this morning."

"I hope you're not counting on me," Casey said, slightly panicky. "I'm not a great cook, either."

"What are you good at, Turner?" Emily asked.

Despite the fact he just wanted to escape, he could see they were both in a little over their heads.

Casey looked inordinately pleased that he had been identified as a chauvinist, though her pleasure seemed short-lived when she realized she was going to have to share the kitchen with him.

"I'm pretty good at breaking eggs," he said. Since he had to suck it up, anyway, Turner could show her a thing or two in the kitchen. He set down his coffee, found a carton of eggs in the fridge and a big bowl under one of the counters.

"Harper, would you stop?" he growled, as the dog stuck her nose in every cupboard he opened. He glanced around the kitchen. Where to set up? Casey obviously did not want him anywhere near her.

But she'd started it! That was where the available counter space was, anyway, so he went and set up there, trying to ignore her glare and the shower-fresh scent of her ticking his nose.

"How many eggs do you want?" he called over his shoulder to Emily.

"Let's see, there will be six of us, plus Carol, and I'll invite Martin in, too. Plus Tessa, so we should do three-egg omelets for the guys, two-egg ones for the women, and a one-egg omelet for Tessa."

Harper whined.

"And a little left over for the dog," Emily said with a smile. It looked as if she was going to have to go for a piece of paper and a pen to figure it out, so Casey took pity on her.

"Twenty-two eggs," she said, "which means one for the dog. Not that I think Carol would approve."

"Maybe not of me inviting Martin, either, though he's good for her. She'd resent me saying so, but Carol seems much happier when he's around," Emily noted with satisfaction. "Love is in the air here at the inn."

Casey hunkered down and stared hard at the cheese grater. Turner tried not to flinch. Had anyone been looking out the window at them skating?

He shot Emily a glance. No, there was no guile in that girl, and even if there was, he didn't have to worry about Casey. It was obvious, after he'd rejected her kiss, she had her defenses up against him. Good!

And it was also obvious she had defenses now. She'd had none back then on the night of Emily and Cole's wedding, and in the days that had followed. And he was not going to wonder what had changed her. He wasn't!

No, he was going to do what he did best: do the job he'd been assigned, quickly and efficiently, and then leave the kitchen. He wasn't going to think about the fact that women didn't generally have their defenses up against him.

He glanced at Casey.

And remembered last night when he had said to her, "Are you happy?"

She hadn't really answered, but she had not been able to hide the stricken look on her face, either.

For a while, out there skating, she had looked happy. And before the fiasco of the kiss, he had been deeply gratified by that.

So, what if he made that part of his assignment this morning? To take the high road? To remember the girl she had been, a long time ago, a too-big, pure white terry-cloth robe wrapped around her, jumping on a king-size bed? To remember the look on her face when he had knelt before her and painted her toenails candy-apple red?

He was good at missions. Surely he could leave his own ghosts behind him long enough to show her that even the most mundane thing could be fun?

His parents had showed him that. The kitchen had been a playground for them. His dad chasing his mom with a towel, tossing eggs around like a professional circus juggler, the dog underfoot...

For the first time, Turner was aware of remembering his parents with a sense of the gift they had given him, rather than all he had lost.

He needed to forget the kiss—she obviously now

realized that had been a mistake—and coax a little laughter from Casey, to show her there were no hard feelings, and no benefit in taking life too seriously, either.

Maybe he could learn the lesson at the same time, accept his parents gift! Life had been a way too serious matter for him for way too long.

"Casey," he said in an undertone, "you don't need to be mad at me."

Not even a glance.

"Mad at you? Why would I be mad at you?" Her own low response was said way too sweetly.

"Look, we both know why."

She said nothing.

"Because I hurt your feelings."

"Oh, you mean you hurt my feelings because you *rejected* me?"

"I didn't reject you. I acted sensibly," he hissed. "We're only here for a few days. Neither of us needs that kind of complication."

"I don't need you to decide what I need. You *are* a chauvinist."

"Okay, I am. I admit it. Can you lighten up now? Can we leave it behind us?"

"I already have," she said. Obviously a lie, since she continued to ignore him. He picked an egg out of the container, tossed it high up behind his back and caught it effortlessly over his shoulder.

Casey glanced his way, pursed those delectable

lips disapprovingly and then squinted hard at the cheese she was grating feverishly.

Still, she could not resist casting him a glance when he did it again. He smiled when she looked, but her disapproving frown only deepened.

His proficiency with eggs was a morning-after trick that usually impressed, but Casey rolled her eyes as if he was an eight-year-old boy who had presented her with the unwanted gift of a frog. She turned her shoulder slightly, blocking her view of his escapades.

Of course, except for that kiss, it wasn't the morning after.

Turner was stunned by the heat that thought of morning afters created in him: waking up beside her, to that wild tangle of curls cascading across a pillow, her olive skin dark against white sheets, her eyes darker than dark with hunger and wanting....

Stop, he ordered himself. If it was about making her smile, there was no room in there for thoughts of morning afters. Or kisses.

He was a highly disciplined man. He needed to prove that.

"Hey, Casey, catch!"

She turned just in time to catch the egg he tossed at her.

"Nice and light," he said approvingly of her catch. "It's like life. You try to hold it too hard, it breaks and you end up with the very thing you were trying to hold on to running through your fingers."

"Oh," she said, and tossed the egg back to him. "The philosopher king. Who would have known?"

He caught the egg easily, spotted a glimmer of a smile as she turned back to her cheese.

Having seen that faint smile, he felt encouraged to clown around a little, amazed that he still had a part of him that could do so. By coaxing that part of her that he had glimpsed long ago back to the surface, he found a lighter part of himself.

He juggled two eggs, and then three. Casey actually stopped to watch him. So did Emily.

Naturally, being a guy, their attention drove him to new heights, literally. He tossed the eggs higher and higher. And then missed.

One splatted on the floor; he tried to catch the next one and it broke in his hand; the third whizzed by him to explode spectacularly against a cupboard door. He never missed. It had to be these sleepless nights catching up with him.

"We love the juggler best when he fumbles," Emily said.

Turner was not sure he wanted the word *love* bandied about when he was anywhere in the vicinity of Casey, with his judgment badly clouded by sleep deprivation.

"It's like life," Casey said. "You toss it around

too lightly and you end up with it running, rather messily, through your fingers."

Harper was thrilled with the fumble, and began to lap eagerly at the mess at Turner's feet.

"She prefers her omelet uncooked," he dead-panned, reaching for a cloth to clean his hands.

And then Casey laughed. It was everything he had hoped for when he had set out to entertain her: the ever-present worry line gone from her forehead, the slight downturn gone from her mouth, the stern disapproval gone from her eyes.

She was lovely, and Turner felt a desire, probably a foolish one, to hear that laugh again. He hoped one more time would be enough.

And another desire, even more foolish, was to finish what they had started this morning, to show her what she had been playing with when she had kissed him that way. It wasn't some dream out of a sweet-sixteen journal.

It was a prelude.

Which was exactly why there would be no kissing, Turner warned himself. That was well outside the parameters of his mission, which was to get Casey to lighten up.

Since he had managed to break the ice, Turner followed his juggling act, after he cleaned up the mess, by breaking the eggs one-handed, dropping the white and yolk from increasing heights into the bowl.

He shook himself, annoyed with the direction his thoughts had taken. Even though she was not the young, inexperienced girl she had been when he'd first met her, she was still not the kind of woman a guy should have those thoughts about.

Casey was intense, not a girl you could kiss lightly or playfully, unless you wanted to go to hell.

But then again, he reminded himself, he had already been there.

Just to be ornery, because after he'd coaxed that laugh out of her she seemed more eager to resist his charms than ever, he *made* her engage with him, still amazed that there was anything in him that could be this light.

Or maybe it wasn't in him. Maybe it was her. Maybe there was something about Casey that had always inspired what was best about him to rise to the surface.

"I was the boy you didn't like getting as a science project partner, wasn't I?"

"I didn't like getting any boy as my science project partner. I'm sure you would have been as good as any of the other ones. Eager to be my partner because you were guaranteed an A and wouldn't have to do any of the work."

"You were cynical very young," he said sadly.

"And frankly, nothing has happened since to change my mind."

Oh, boy, she was just not going to let him off the

hook for what she saw as his defection all those years ago.

All that had happened a long, long time ago. And it hadn't been his fault. He would show her his charming side, and was willing to bet she would forgive him by the time the omelets were up.

"So, Casey," he said casually, getting back to the conversation he'd had with her last night. "What makes you happy? Tell me what you do for fun."

What surprised him was that he really wanted to know.

She glared at him as if he had asked for a peek of her underwear. "I take yoga," she offered reluctantly.

"I've always wanted to try that."

She pursed her lips in disapproval at the lie. "No, you haven't."

He debated telling her about the hazards of frown marks, and decided against it. For now.

"I heard it was great for strength and flexibility." Not to mention the counselor it was mandatory he see right now, because of that gong show on the other side of the world, had told him he should give it a shot. To find *peace*.

Peace was a word that was bandied around a lot. It was supposedly the reason men went to war. Was he the only person who saw how ridiculous that was? Not that it had seemed ridiculous when he was a young man intent on changing the world in honor of his father.

Still, that promise had made him check a yoga class schedule, but he had never quite made it through the doors. The advertisements for the class had showed young women in tights turning their bodies into pretzels.

"Are there any men in your yoga class?" he asked.

"While some of the best yoga masters are men, in my experience," she said primly, "most men aren't good at yoga. They fall asleep during *savasana*. And snore. And they—" She stopped, began to grate cheese with a vengeance.

"They what?"

"You shouldn't eat before doing yoga," she said, not looking up, "or at least not a ten-ounce steak and a pound of fries. Men never seem to get that."

She shredded cheese; he glanced at her. She was blushing! What would be making her blush about men eating full meals before yoga? Suddenly, he got it, and hooted with laughter.

"Are you telling me you have some flatulent Freddy in your yoga class?"

"It's not funny," she warned him.

"Not even a little bit?"

"Ten-year-old boys find flatulence funny," she said cuttingly, "not full-grown men."

"That shows how many full-grown men you

know," he retorted, grinning, hoping to tug a smile out of her.

But she gave him a scathing look, obviously intent on not letting him get her guard down again, and returned to her work.

He should warn her just to give up now. He was on a mission, after all.

"What does *shavasana* mean?"

"Death or corpse pose," she said.

"That's what you do for *fun?*" He was glad he had never made it through the doors of a yoga class. He was searching for peace, yes; death he had seen quite enough of. Especially in Beza-zabur, the worst mission of his career. They had known, going in, the odds were against them. The mission had succeeded, but at an enormous price. He could feel the sadness of loss of good men tugging at him, and tried to shake it off.

"It's a relaxation pose, at the end of class." Casey was watching him closely, as if she knew something had shifted in him.

He pasted on his grin, not liking the sensation of being stripped, as if she could see his soul.

"Well, yoga just doesn't sound fun. Flatulent Freddy falls asleep during it. I've never known a single person to fall asleep while having fun. I always wondered if downward dog had any potential."

Harper's tail thumped happily at the word *dog*.

"For what?" Casey asked suspiciously.

"Fun. It's got that sound about it." He wiggled his eyebrows at her.

"It's downward-facing dog," she said, but she was still watching him closely, as if she detected he was trying to use humor to slip away from something too intense. "And it's a strength and balance pose."

"Not fun?" he said sadly.

"I think you can eliminate yoga as a source of fun," she said.

"So, what else, then?"

"Pardon?"

She had the snootiest look on her face. Snooty people said "pardon?" instead of "huh?" or "what?"

That expression was endearing for a reason he could not decipher.

"For fun?" he reminded her. "Now that Freddy has destroyed the serenity of yoga class, and you've said yourself it has little potential, what else do you do for fun?"

She was silent.

"Didn't you say you were taking calligraphy?" Emily said helpfully.

"Calligraphy?"

"Not for fun," Casey said defensively. "It helps me relax."

"Look, maybe it's not for me to say—"

"It's not!" she exclaimed, almost panic-stricken at having her ultraboring life exposed.

"But I think you are getting quite enough relaxation in the *shavasana* department."

The cheese grater was put down. She folded her arms across her chest. "And what would you suggest for fun, Mr. Kennedy? Since you are apparently some kind of expert on the subject."

He ordered his eyes not to veer to her mouth. They did anyway.

She licked her lips uneasily, then, realizing what she had done, pulled her cute little tongue back in her mouth and pressed her lips into a straight line.

She regarded him solemnly, and then said, in a low voice Emily couldn't hear, "Why do I get the impression, for all your talk, it's been a long time since you found life fun, Turner Kennedy?"

"You seemed to enjoy skating with me this morning," he said. "We should try that again. As long as we both understand the limits."

She actually blushed at the reference to her uninvited advance, but looked as haughty as ever at the very same time.

"I understand Andrea has a very ambitious plan for the next few days, so why don't we just leave it for now?"

He stared at her.

Casey Caravetta had just said no to him!

CHAPTER EIGHT

CASEY CARAVETTA HAD said no to him, and Turner told himself just to be grateful. Damned grateful. She'd picked up that particular lesson very quickly.

He'd always known she was about the smartest girl in the world. No doubt she had seen straight through the act—the egg juggling and the one-handed breakage—to the damage beneath.

The damage that would make a man refuse a pretty girl's kiss. For her own damn good.

"Forget I asked," he said gruffly.

And he didn't like the way she was gazing at him, too closely.

"Did I hurt your feelings now?" she asked softly.

Okay, his head was starting to hurt. There were just way too many *feelings* being bandied about.

He shot her a look. "No, you didn't."

She appeared skeptical and sympathetic.

"You can't hurt my feelings."

"Oh, right," she said in a wounded tone. "The

girl you can reject has no power over you. How silly of me."

"I thought we left that behind us? You can't hurt my feelings because I don't have any feelings to hurt."

She looked at him, and the sympathy in her eyes deepened. "You can't possibly believe that."

"Believe it? I know it."

She looked sympathetic and then exasperated. But it was like reading an open book. He could tell the moment she realized it wasn't safe to sympathize with him.

"I'm sorry," she said primly, just as if he had said she *had* hurt his feelings. "My not wanting to skate anymore is not about you. It's about me."

He knew a dig when he heard it.

"We don't want things to get complicated, after all," she said sweetly.

"Let's get something straight. Skating and kissing are not the same thing."

"Thanks, Sherlock, now I won't have to look them up in my dictionary."

"I just thought maybe you'd like to have some fun."

"And I need you to do that?"

"Are you always this aggravating?"

For a second, from the spark in her eye, he thought she might just demonstrate true aggravation by throwing the cheese grater at his head.

Sadly, she regained control and stepped back from the counter.

"There's enough cheese here for ten omelets, Emily. If you'll excuse me, I have wild adventures awaiting me in the fun department."

"Ha. Rereading *War and Peace?*" Turner muttered.

Casey cast him one more disparaging look. "At least I know how to read."

Emily was watching his reaction as Casey marched by him, nose in the air, and out the swinging kitchen door.

"I don't think she handles being teased very well, Turner."

He turned and gave her his toothiest grin. "I was just trying to be friendly. Who would have thought discussing yoga class could be dangerous?"

"My, my. It's been a long time since anyone said no to you, hasn't it, Turner Kennedy?"

He kept the grin. "The week is young."

"Don't play with her, Turner." Emily bit her lip. "Casey's having a bit of a tough time right now."

He wasn't quite sure why, but he didn't like thinking of Casey having a tough time.

"Why?"

Em hesitated, decided to trust him. "We all lost our friend Melissa this year. Casey also had a breakup. And her dad died."

"Poor kid," he said, surprised by how genuine his sympathy was.

"I don't think she'd appreciate you seeing her as a kid."

"Gotcha."

"Something else is going on. Some reason she doesn't want to spend Christmas with her mom. It seems odd. Her mom's first Christmas alone." Emily shook her head. "It just seems as if it's the wrong time for Casey to be making such a major life decision."

Something prickled along the back of Turner's neck. "What major life decision?" he asked softly.

Emily laughed uneasily. "I shouldn't have said that. I don't think she'd appreciate me mulling over her personal life with a guy she barely knows."

He thought back to the night of Emily and Cole's wedding. Somehow it did feel as if he knew Casey Caravetta, though he knew that assessment was not completely rational.

"So," Emily said, with a soft smile, "don't play with her, but don't give up on her, either."

And as soon as Em said that, he realized he had already decided he wasn't going to.

Give up on Casey. A long time ago he should have sent her a note and hadn't. Was it ever too late to do the right thing?

The play-with-her part was a whole different story.

He took his bowl of eggs, placed them in front of Emily and walked out of the kitchen in search of the uncomplicated companionship of Cole.

Turner's uncomplicated companion, Harper, followed him loyally.

But when Casey didn't appear for breakfast, Turner felt honor bound to track her down.

"Come on, open the door."

"No," she called through the door. "I'm just getting to the really fun part of *War and Peace*."

"There are no fun parts in war. I know from experience." He wished, instantly, that he hadn't said that. "You missed breakfast. I brought you an omelet."

She opened the door and looked at him cautiously. He suspected the door had been opened because he'd let it slip he had firsthand experience with war. He wanted to make her life lighter, not evoke her sympathy.

"I don't want the omelet."

"It's only fair, after all the cheese you grated. Come on. The dog is tormenting me, thinking it's for her."

Harper whined helpfully, as if on cue.

"You've had enough eggs for one day," Turner told her.

Casey folded her arms over her chest, glaring at him. "What part of no don't you get?"

He wafted the steaming omelet under her nose.

"You're not used to women saying no to you, are you?"

"You and Emily are onto me."

"Harper," she said, addressing the dog firmly, "stop fawning over him. You're a disgrace."

"I promise I won't see it as fawning over me if you take the omelet."

"And then you'll go away?"

He nodded insincerely and handed her the plate. She took it, then set it on a dresser beside the door and crossed her arms over her chest again.

He saw it as hopeful that she hadn't slammed the door.

"I'm waiting for the going-away part," she said.

She planned to resist his attempts to lighten up a life that seemed to have got bogged down in seriousness. He planned not to let her. For the first time in a long time, he felt almost lighthearted.

He leaned his shoulder against her doorjamb. "I like your hair like that."

"Humph. I just haven't had time to do anything with it yet today."

"Can I touch it?"

"No." She began to ease the door shut. He slid his foot in. She glared.

"You missed all the discussion at breakfast. Andrea is handing out assignments like crazy. The vow renewal is going to be on the steps of the front porch, with the guests seated in a semicircle on chairs below it. She and Carol are making garlands out of real boughs. And wreaths. Cole and Martin are replacing the old Christmas light strings with new ones, LEDs to save the inn money. And you and I—"

"You and I?" she asked, nonplussed.

He nodded.

"How did I end up with you?" she asked suspiciously.

"It was your lucky day?" The truth was most women would have been delighted to have been paired with him. "Look, Casey, we're the only two single people here. I think it's natural we're going to end up together from time to time. Can we declare a truce?"

"What job did we get?"

"Andrea has this idea that it would be fun to have an honor guard of snowmen at the front gate."

"What? A snowman honor guard?"

The wariness faded from her face. She looked, however reluctantly, enchanted by the concept.

"FYI, it doesn't get any hokier," he told her. He had been tempted to tell Andrea that he wasn't sure about messing with such tradition as the military arch ceremony, but then he had reminded himself that if he wanted to help Casey lighten up, he was going to have to do a little lightening up himself.

"It's cute!"

"Adorable," he said drily.

"And also very economical. It's very smart of Andrea to use something free, like snow. Her budget for turning this place into a winter wonderland is limited."

Somehow he didn't think he would win any points for saying he thought the budget *should* be limited, for a one-day event that had no real, pragmatic purpose.

"Can you meet me in the front yard in half an hour?"

"That doesn't give me time to do my hair!"

Good, he thought. Out loud, he said, "There is no sense doing your hair for snowman duty. It's probably going to end up wet. Stuff it under a hat."

Obviously, she was torn between outright refusing to help him, and giving in. And he suspected, when she gave in, it had nothing to do with his considerable egg-juggling charm. The snowmen were luring her.

"I'll see you down there, then." And she shut the door quietly in his face.

Turner stood there for a moment longer. It occurred to him he had actually been holding his breath, waiting for her answer.

It occurred to him she had said yes to building snowmen, not to the truce.

CHAPTER NINE

CASEY LEANED AGAINST the door. Hard as it was to admit it, Turner was right. They had to declare a truce. She could not let him get under her skin. If he got under her skin, she could not let him know it!

And, of course, he already had got to her this morning, tossing eggs at her, throwing them around. She had actually laughed when he had broken them, that astonished look on his face saying he couldn't believe he had fumbled.

Sadly, she could not remember the last time she had enjoyed such a good chuckle!

She had come here to find something: a part of herself that could be at peace with her life if she remained single forever.

The truth? Yoga and calligraphy weren't doing it, but she was sure that motherhood would.

Something had drawn her to the inn, as if there was an answer here. In simplicity. In friendships. In the spirit of Christmas itself. These were things she wanted for her child!

And she wasn't going to find that answer locked in her room, hiding from Turner Kennedy and his considerable charms. He was the test, dammit, and she intended to pass it!

She had to give herself over to what the day held, and today that was making snowmen.

And she had to admit, reluctantly, that it did sound fun. It was something she would want to do with her child one day.

And just as reluctantly, she had to admit that somehow Turner had hit the nail right on the head when he had insinuated that fun might be the missing element from her life. What kind of mom would she be if she couldn't just have fun?

Putting her pride aside—she would need her strength, after all—Casey gobbled down the omelet he had brought and then turned her attention to the all-important matter of what to wear for snowman building.

Half an hour later, feeling like a large pink marshmallow in the snowsuit that had seemed so "fun" when she had bought it for this trip, and which now seemed faintly ridiculous, Casey headed out the front door of the inn. She had stuffed every strand of her wildly uncooperative hair under a knit hat that looked like an exaggerated version of what a hippie out of the sixties would have worn.

The sun had come out and made the snow sparkle with a million diamond lights. It was a fairy-land of delight.

Turner was already outside, pacing out large steps. He had out a tape measure and ran it from the arbor at the front gate to the stairs. Harper marched up and down beside him, dogging his every step.

"Would you go away?" he said to the dog.

Harper pondered this, decided she had been ordered to sit, and sat down on his foot.

He glared at the dog, but indulgently, and let the tape roll up as Casey came toward him.

"I was thinking eight," he said, "four on each side. But I don't think we have room for them. Not if the chairs start, say, right here."

"Eight snowmen?"

"Too ambitious?"

"Way."

"Well, that's a relief. How about four, two on each side?"

"I hope you know how to build a snowman."

"If I can juggle eggs, I can build a snowman."

"Hmm, I'm not following the relationship between the two, but I'm going to trust you have actually built one before."

"Who hasn't?" he said, frowning down at his tape measure. Her silence made him look up and transfer his frown to her.

"You've never built a snowman?" He seemed astounded by that.

"I grew up in an apartment in New York, so snowmen were not part of my experience."

"You didn't go to the park?"

She shrugged, but could feel him looking at her intently.

"You didn't have a childhood at all, did you?" he said suddenly, his voice husky and deep. "Your brother's illness stole all that from you, didn't it?"

Why did he remember that? Was it just part of his considerable charm? How did she play this game? Give herself over to having fun at the same time as protecting herself from Turner Kennedy?

Casey felt terribly vulnerable all at once, standing there in the pink snowsuit she had never owned as a child. As if she was going to either burst into tears or run.

How could she hope to be a good mother when nothing about her own childhood had given her the kind of experiences she would need?

"I'll show you," he said, way too gently. "I'll show you how to build a snowman, Casey."

She swallowed hard, and said with stiff pride that hid the gratitude blooming in her heart, "I'm sure it's not rocket science."

"Or science of any kind, which puts you at a disadvantage." He smirked, the sympathy gone, or mercifully hidden. "Now watch. Step one." He scooped up a generous mittful of snow. "This stuff is absolutely perfect for it. Not too dry. Not too wet. Slightly sticky, like the rice you make sushi rolls with."

"I suppose you do that, too?" she asked skeptically, watching him form the snow into a smooth, perfect ball.

"What?"

"Make sushi rolls."

"It's easier than you think. And it impresses, er, people."

But she got it. It impressed women people. And no doubt juggling eggs did, also. The touch of aggravation that made her feel—Turner Kennedy, dark, dangerous and suave, the man no woman could resist—was far superior to the way she had felt when he had guessed her brother's death had stolen her childhood.

"You do it, too," he said, holding out his snowball for her inspection.

She scooped up a mitten of snow, clamped her hands around it and watched it squish out either side.

"Make a round ball. Like this." He set his snowball down, scooped up more snow, placed it in her mittens and guided her hands around it. "Pat, don't squeeze."

She wanted to keep her guard up against the man who knew how to make sushi to impress, but it was very hard with his hands wrapped around hers. She kept losing herself in his intensity about the correct procedure for building snowballs.

Was he that serious? Or was he just pretending? It would do very well to remember it was hard to tell when Turner Kennedy was pretending and when he wasn't!

"Hey, Casey, this step is more important than you think. A mistake here could result in a square snowman."

"Maybe we could start a trend," she suggested innocently.

"You can mess with your hair if you have to, but don't mess with snowmen."

She obediently patted the snow together, under his watchful eye. She peeked up at him. He wasn't watching her hands, but her face, a little smile of pleasure on his lips.

She held up the result and he inspected it carefully, standing way too close to her. She found his scent intoxicating, part of the clean crispness of a fresh wintry morning.

"You're a natural," he decided, as he pulled a glove off one hand with his teeth. "Hey, some of your hair is escaping. Wouldn't want that! Like a nun letting some come free of her wimple."

"I told you I was sensitive on the topic of nuns right now," she said, and knew it was a weakness when, despite the mutinous expression on her face, she allowed him to push the little tendrils of hair back under her cap with his ungloved fingers. "What's a wimple?"

"That white thing that surrounds their face. And that is just about the full extent of my knowledge about nuns."

"Thank heaven for small mercies."

"Are you going to tell me why you're sensitive to the subject of nuns right now?"

"No."

"Seriously, I'm intrigued."

"Isn't that just the story of my life," she muttered.

"What?"

"Whenever somebody's intrigued by me, it's always for the wrong reasons."

"Oh. What would you like me to be intrigued about?"

Whether she put bubbles in her bath. What kind of flowers she would prefer sent on her birthday.

"I already know what your underwear looks like, after all. Caught a peek of it when your suitcase fell open."

"Oh, never mind," she said a touch grouchily.

He eyed her. For a man who knew how to make sushi to impress, he seemed a little stupid in the what-to-be-intrigued-about department.

"I'm intrigued about why you aren't married," he said, cocking his head and considering her. "Geez. I hope that's not the connection. You aren't considering becoming a nun, are you?"

"Maybe I am," she said.

"The underwear says no."

"It's old. The new me is more practical." He had sucked her into discussing something very personal with him. She thought he would snort with satisfaction, but he didn't. In fact, he eyed her narrowly.

"Some bastard hurt you."

Her mouth gaped open and then snapped shut.

"When?" he said.

"I haven't even confirmed that!"

"You don't have to. I can tell." He gave himself a little smack on the forehead. "The clues were all there. Yoga and calligraphy. The new revelation about practical undies. Sheesh. You're practically a nun already."

She opened her mouth to protest, to tell him she was going to have a child, not become a nun, but she shut it again, thankful she had regained control, since she did not want that truth about herself open to his dissection.

"When?"

"It's nearly a year ago. I'm so over it."

"Humph," he said, with insulting disbelief.

"I am!" Again there was a temptation to share with him just how she was getting on with her life, but once more she battled it down.

"What did he do?"

"Could we just build the snowman?"

"Okay," he said, tugging his glove back on with

his teeth—was he doing that on purpose making her focus on his all too sexy mouth? "But this is not over."

"What if I say it is?"

He shrugged.

"You're infuriating."

He smiled. "Yes, I am. Okay, set that extraordinary sample of the beginnings of a snowman on the ground and roll it, before you crush it between your fingers pretending it is my head."

She pretended it was his head and set it on the ground, gave it a very vigorous shove.

He sighed. "I'll show you with mine, first."

The dog tried to help him with her nose.

"A little bit this way and then a little bit that way," he instructed. "Harper! So it stays nice and round. Only we'll start on this side of the yard and roll toward the archway so we don't have to move them too far when they're the right size."

Casey watched him for a moment or two. There was something about watching a male apply all that muscle and strength to this task that was at least as lovely as watching him clear snow from the lake and chop wood. Harper's dedication to him was endearing, too. Weren't dogs supposed to be good judges of character?

Then Turner caught her looking, and winked!

Blushing, annoyed with herself, she dropped her own ball of snow and began to push it, first one way, then another. In no time she was totally engrossed in her task, tongue caught between teeth, grunting with exertion, hat askew and hair falling out of it.

The snowball, she saw with pleasure, had picked up every ounce of snow in its wildly weaving path, leaving a trail of naked brown grass in its wake. It was becoming astonishingly large in a very short amount of time. She had to get down on her knees to push it.

"Hey, is that downward-facing dog?" he teased.

"Downward-facing, sweating dog," she said, then gave a mighty push and ended up on her face. He roared with laughter as she sat up, brushing snow off her cheeks and clothes.

"Here, you'll need some 'mus-cull' for this part," he said, making a fist and curling his arm to show her who had the "mus-culls." Even under his jacket, his muscle popped up cooperatively. Casey told herself she was having trouble breathing only because of the heavy exertion of the exercise.

To let him know she was not impressed, and that her heavy breathing had nothing to do with him or his childish display of strength, she rolled her eyes. "A man who quotes Popeye."

"I like a girl who knows her Popeye," he said.

But when he dropped down on his knees beside her, she knew exactly why her heart was beating way too hard. And worse, she surrendered something, as if his closeness was a drug and she was hopelessly addicted.

She surrendered her need to be in control.

She let go of her tight hold on her desire to protect herself.

She did something she had not done in far too long. She gave herself permission to have fun. And she had a feeling it wasn't just for the sake of her future children!

She took the hat off her too-hot head and tossed it aside. Aware of his eyes on her, she shook out the curls.

"Whoa," he muttered, "when you have hair like that you can be practical in every other respect!"

He thought she was sexy. And she had no idea what to do with that!

Thankfully, he tore his eyes away from her freed locks, and put his shoulder to the huge snow boulder. She settled beside him, and together, shoulder to shoulder, with the dog bouncing along, barking and trying to figure out how to insert herself between them, they pushed it into place beside the arch in the fence.

"Okay," he said, "we're on a roll—no pun intended—so now is not the time to rest on our laurels." He deliberately glanced at the "laurels" she was resting on, grinned wolfishly and then raced back and began to maneuver the next ball across the yard. She joined him, huffing, puffing, giggling, slipping.

She noticed with relief that her self-consciousness dissipated as she gave herself over to the pure fun of being on the same team as him.

His shoulder was right against hers. They were pushing together. Their shouts and laughter filled the air.

His feet slipped, the ball trundled away from him and he flipped over on his back, panting. She lay down beside him and for a moment they both watched wispy clouds float through a bright blue winter sky.

Peripherally, she was aware of Carol and Andrea on the porch, making garlands out of a huge heap of evergreen boughs, and fastening them to the railings. Cole and Martin were on the roof, taking down old strings of light.

All that was in the background, but still, she had a sense of being part of something. A little community of people who wanted to make things wonderful for Cole and Emily.

"It feels so good," Turner said quietly. "I feel as if I lived to have a moment like this."

"Me, too," she whispered, and realized they were two people who had come through the battlefields of life to arrive at this moment of utter delight. Of peace. She realized she had laughed out loud.

She had given herself totally to the present moment, something yoga urged her to do, and she had never quite succeeded at until now.

And she knew you had to take those moments when they were offered. It occurred to her that maybe she and Turner had declared a truce, after all.

Just when she thought the moment could not be any more perfect, he reached over, took her hand and squeezed it firmly, letting her know he felt it, too.

They were on the same wavelength.

Just like they had been all those years ago.

He turned his head to her, gazed at her through the sooty abundance of his lashes. She wondered, her heart beating in her throat, if he was going to kiss her.

He leaned close. Against her better judgment, she did, too. She could feel her eyelids drop. Her mouth puckered.

"So," he said huskily, so close to her his breath stirred her hair, "tell me what he did."

CHAPTER TEN

CASEY REELED BACK from Turner. She set her mouth in a straight line and opened her eyes wide, in a glare. So much for the truce!

Just like all those years ago, he was winning her trust, stealing her secrets from her. To what end?

And that thought spoiled the present moment completely for her. She let go of his hand, found her feet and went back to her next snowball.

"Look," Turner said silkily, "it's probably not even that original. What he did."

"Would you please stop?"

He pursed his lips together grudgingly.

Still, they had to cooperate somewhat, even if it was in silence, to wrestle two large balls to one side of the walkway and two on the other. Since he didn't mention it again, she decided to forgive him in the name of teamwork. Plus, there was something lighter in him. There had been since he had tossed those eggs that morning. It was as if he was making a deliberate effort to push away some shadow.

And she had a feeling the effort was for her. How could you turn down a gift like that, even if Turner was just about the most aggravating man on the planet?

They began to roll the middle balls, slightly smaller, that would form the tummies of their snowmen. They lifted those into place, and she stood panting, regarding their handiwork, as he cemented those second boulders into place by jamming snow where they joined.

"We're good," she decided. She slid him a look. *We.*

"That's right," he said, "a team."

A team. As in her and him. Was it dangerous to be thinking of them as some kind of team? Definitely.

"We're not a team," she said. "We're just two people thrown together in an attempt to make two other people happy."

"There are worse reasons to be thrown together," he said, "Take you and old what's his name—"

He laughed at the grimace she made, then bent, caught up a handful of snow and tossed it in her face. "Lighten up, Doc."

She noticed they were alone in the yard now. Everyone else had gone in. Maybe it was the fact that there was no audience that made her feel so uninhibited.

She spluttered and wiped it away. Glared at his grinning face, Casey bent, scooped up her own handful of snow and stalked toward him with menace.

"Chicken," she called as he made a run for it, then turned and looked at her, ducking this way and that, making it very hard to aim.

"What? You think I'm going to stand there and let you throw snow in my face?"

"You can run, but you cannot hide," she said, and gave chase. She let fly with her snow, shrieked with disappointment when it fell well short of him. He snickered happily. In the time it took her to form a new weapon, he hit her twice with fat wet snowballs.

"This is war!" she declared.

"Bring it," he challenged her, and bring it she did.

Screeching with wild abandon, she chased him around the yard, trying to hit him with snowballs. Only one of hers landed for every six of his.

Finally, panting, she leaned her hands on her knees. She wasn't quite sure how, but somehow while chasing him around the yard, pure frustration had become something else completely.

Joyous. As if she was playing, in a way she never had as a child.

Deliberately, hiding snow behind her back, she fell over and cried out. "Turner!"

"What?" He raced to her side, all playfulness gone.

"I think I twisted my ankle."

"Let me look."

Without hesitation, he sank down in the snow beside her, yanked up the leg of her snow pants. He was scowling with intense concentration, trying to get through the layers of snowsuit and socks and boots to her ankle.

Giggling with evil delight, she yanked her foot away and shoved snow down his back. He shook it out, but when she went to find her feet and scamper away from him, he snagged her ankle and she fell back in the snow.

He flipped her over and straddled her, pinning her arms.

"That was wicked," he said, with a certain amount of approval. "But you know what happens to the girl who cries wolf, don't you?"

Casey squirmed underneath him and then gazed up into his face. He looked, right now, like the boy she had once known, his eyes alight with laughter, and she felt her heart go still.

Suddenly, it didn't seem funny at all as he stared down at her.

"What?" she whispered.

She didn't feel playful. Or peaceful, for that matter.

But she did feel more alive than she had in a long, long time. Could feel the beat of her own heart. Feel air that was scented of him touching her skin, then being drawn inside her, pulled deep within her lungs. Feel the easy strength of his legs, pinning her to the ground.

"I forget," he said, then put his hands on both sides of her face. Her sense of being trapped by him was deliciously complete. And then he dropped his mouth over hers.

Casey met his lips, tasted them and him. What she tasted on his lips was pure, as sparkling as the diamond-crusted snow all around them.

And what she tasted of him was also pure, his essence: strength and playfulness, depth and courage.

He sighed with satisfaction when his gloved hands found her hair, tangled in it, used it to draw himself down even more.

Something unleashed within her as he pulled her in, their snow-damp clothes sticking together. They were generating a world of heat. She wouldn't be surprised to pull away from him and find the snow melted and spring arriving in a ten-foot radius around them!

Then his lips parted hers with tender command, and his tongue explored the soft inner swell there, the hard edge of her upper teeth. And then it darted into the hollow of her mouth.

The potential for meltdown increased. So did the feeling of being intensely alive.

Casey felt as if the blood was turning hot in her veins, and his energy was melding with her own. She could feel herself surrendering despite her every vow not to surrender to this.

It took an iron will to remind herself she had lured him to her because she was losing the snow-ball fight.

It appeared that if she didn't smarten up now, she was going to lose this other battle, too.

From under the fog of feeling, she allowed a memory of past hurt to surface and strengthen her spine.

She retook control, though she was aware she did it with a sense of loss rather than triumph.

He had loosened his grip on her hands, and she grabbed snow from either side of her and shoved it down his neck.

Turner gave a shout of surprised outrage and leaped off her. He performed a little break dance she might have found hilarious if she wasn't still reeling from the power of what had just transpired between them.

He shook the snow out of his shirt and shot her a dark look that made her shiver.

"You don't play fair," he told her.

"All's fair in love and war," she retorted, and instantly regretted using both words around him.

"Yes, it is," he said with satisfaction.

She frowned at him.

"Because let me tell you something, Casey Caravetta."

She waited.

"I found out exactly what I needed to know."

She cocked her head, raised an eyebrow in what she hoped could be interpreted as amusement.

"You," he said softly, "aren't ever going to be a nun."

She dropped any pretense of amusement and glared at him.

"And something else?"

She folded her arms over her chest with what she hoped to pass off as complete indifference.

"It had nothing to do with you. Him cheating on you."

Her mouth fell open. "How could you possibly know that? From a kiss?"

He grinned. "I didn't. The nun part was from the kiss. The other part was just a guess. But I did tell you it probably wasn't even original."

"Consider this truce over!" she said. The source of her intense pain was not even *original*?

"It's not like you did anything to deserve it."

"The truce?"

"The cad."

It was the absolution she had never been willing to

give herself, and she felt driven to let Turner know it was her fault. Who had picked him, after all?

"It hurt my pride, okay? I should have been smarter than that! I was engaged to him and never caught on to his deceit. A coworker had a little chat with me."

It was spilling out of her like water against a weakened dam. She realized Turner had sucked her into talking about it.

"Better a bit of hurt pride than a life of misery," he said softly.

"You don't get it! I can't trust myself to make the right choices." She thought of her choice to have a baby on her own. "About men!"

Casey turned and stomped away from him, focused on the snow.

She managed to channel all her angry energy into making snowmen. Without speaking another word to each other they had four snowmen guarding the gate and the walkway by lunchtime.

Turner walked around them, apparently unperturbed by her silent treatment. He was inspecting their morning's handiwork with deep masculine pleasure, picking a leaf or tuft of grass out here and there, smoothing the snow with a gloved hand.

"They look a little naked," she ventured at last, breaking her silence. She reminded herself it was asking for it to use the word *naked* around a guy like him. He'd probably tease her until she blushed.

He didn't rise to the bait. Casey tried to tell herself she was pleased about that, but instead decided he must like the distance between them.

And was sorry he had given in to the temptation to kiss her, when he had resisted so successfully on the frozen lake.

"Andrea told me she got some top hats from the five and dime, and some cheap vests and neckties," Turner said. "She doesn't want to get them out until the twenty-fourth, though, in case we get more snow."

Casey realized from just a few minutes of standing still that her snowsuit was soaked through and her extremities were freezing. Turner noticed her shivering and shaking her hands to restore feeling.

"Here." He came over to her. "Let me warm them up."

The temptation of having that happen was too much to resist. She gave him her hand, but with a stern warning. "Just don't mistake this for a truce."

"I got it. A truce has to be sealed with a kiss."

He cupped her frozen hand with both his own. How was it they were still so warm?

Then, her hand clasped in his, he lifted it to his lips and blew on her cold, cold fingertips. They burned at first, and then the most luscious warmth crept into them.

Honestly, it was worse than being kissed, and just as intimate. And just as sensual!

She should have pulled away, but really, she was powerless.

"Better?" he asked.

She could only nod.

He released her hand, took the other and did the same thing, his eyes intent on her face.

"Lots of men are trustworthy," he said, finally.

"Are you?" she whispered.

He dropped her hand as if it was hot, but didn't step away from her. It looked as if he was pondering the question, and of course, she already knew the answer, if somebody had to think that hard!

"Hey, you two, everyone else came in for lunch ages ago. It's getting cold."

Carol was standing on a porch that had been transformed into something out of a dream, the railings covered with an abundance of green boughs with beautiful white bows threaded through them. The innkeeper was watching them, a small smile drifting across her lips.

They pulled apart as if a rubber band had held them and suddenly snapped.

Not looking at each other, shaking off snow, they walked up stairs fragrant with evergreen and past Carol, who never quit smiling as she reached out to give her dog a pat as Harper followed Turner into the house.

CHAPTER ELEVEN

"Ham!" The sound of his own voice startled Turner awake. Had he shouted or whispered?

"We making cookies now. Not ham."

Turner opened one eye warily.

He looked into the face of Tessa, Rick's six-year-old daughter. Her eyes were inches from his, huge and solemn.

"I don't make cookies," he said gruffly. He closed his eyes, a hint for her to leave him alone.

It had caught up with him. Poor sleep, lots of physical activity. Casey, her hair straightened to within an inch of its life, was being frostily polite to him, and avoiding him today, one day after they had built the snowmen and he had pried her life's secrets from her.

Maybe not all her life secrets. Nothing she had said to him yesterday seemed even remotely like the major life decision Emily had mentioned.

Though he'd been able to ascertain she wasn't becoming a nun.

And was still hurting enough over some jerk that she wasn't entering into another bad relationship, either.

I don't trust myself. Around men.

And then the all-important could she trust *him?* It was a complicated question, but she had seen his hesitancy as all the answer she needed.

"We got a Christmas tree," Tessa informed him. "It's outside 'cause it's full of snow."

Over breakfast the group had been making plans to go in search of a Christmas tree in the nearby woods.

Casey's eyes had been shining like a kid about to meet Santa for the first time. And then she had shot him a look and bit her lip.

He knew if he said he was going to get the tree with them, she would have found an excuse not to.

For a girl who thought she had been dumb about men, she seemed to be playing it pretty smart with him. After that steaming kiss between them yesterday, she was putting as much space between them as the close confines of the inn would allow.

Turner knew that was good, of course, really good. He just wasn't sure why he felt so grumpy about it. Probably because a kiss had been way outside the parameters of his stated mission.

Not that that explained why he had felt grumpier yet when Casey had announced she wanted to have her turn with the ax!

What was that about? Obviously, Rick, Tessa's dad, and a fireman to boot, would be an expert on safety with an ax. Turner did not have to be there to make sure Casey didn't cut off her foot.

He needed his sleep way more than he needed to be around a woman as complicated and aggravating as Casey Caravetta. He had taken to the couch as soon as the door had shut behind the tree party.

It was better he didn't go. He was still feeling oddly battered and bruised from the snowman building thing. And not physically, either.

It was as if being around her took a run at all his hard-earned cynicism, uncovered longings that he had not been aware he had.

Not to mention threatened his ability to be in control.

He liked being in control, living by his motto, *If It's Out Of Your Control, You're In Trouble.*

And part of remaining in control was not getting sucked in by the fairy-tale vow renewal and Christmas unfolding at the inn. It wasn't reality. It was a manipulation of reality.

To tell the truth, he regretted whatever altruistic motivation had led him to knock on Casey's bedroom door yesterday and coerce her to come out and build snowmen with him.

He probably could have kept it all very big-brotherly and "Let's help poor solemn Casey have fun" if she would have kept her damned hat on and her luscious lips to herself.

"We making cookies *now*," Tessa insisted. "For the wedding."

He opened his eyes and scowled at her. "You're still here?"

The little mite didn't seem the least intimidated by him. She smiled and nodded.

He sighed. "What wedding?"

"Aunt Emily's."

It wasn't a wedding, exactly, but explaining the distinction to a six-year-old was not in his skill set. "What time is it?"

"I don't know how to tell time."

"Didn't your…" He stopped. She didn't have a mom, and because of that he managed to strip a fragment of the unfriendliness out of his voice. "Didn't your dad tell you not to talk to strangers?"

She took his hand and tugged. "You're not a stranger, Uncle Turner!"

He was not her uncle, and he was tempted to tell her so to dampen her enthusiasm, but again he remembered life had been mean enough to her without him chipping in.

The dog, who had also noticed his opening eyes, was thumping her tail with adoration. Tessa's trust in him, like the dog's, was making Turner feel off-kilter.

He was a warrior, for goodness sake. One look at

him and the dogs were supposed to turn and run, tails curled between their legs. People were supposed to hide their children.

"Come make cookies. Please…?"

"Why me?" he said out loud.

"I like you," Tessa declared with utter sincerity.

"Sheesh."

Turner had a niece a little younger than this that he had never met. His brothers had never said he wasn't welcome home for Christmas, but they'd never told him he was, either.

He tried to disengage his hand from Tessa's, but that just made her hang on more mulishly. He closed his eyes again. Was he getting a headache? His mission had originally been to get Casey to lighten up. Why was it shifting? Now he wanted her to face reality?

"Uncle Turner…!"

Oh, definitely a headache.

"I want to make cookies now. Gingerbread, like in the story. That's my favorite story."

The child's voice was becoming more strident. She looked as if she planned to start yelling if she didn't get her own way. Explaining a screaming child to her buff daddy, the fireman, wasn't in his skill set, either.

"I wanted the big one," Tessa said, and the stridency was gone. Her lower lip trembled. "The big gingerbread man in Andrea's store, but he's gone."

She was two seconds away from crying. Turner's aversion to tears was as strong as ever.

So even though it wasn't in his nature, he'd surrender. And while he was in the kitchen, he'd just have a little peek at Casey. If they were making cookies, no doubt she would be in the thick of it.

Maybe he'd say a few words to her, just to find out if she'd discovered cutting down trees was damned hard work, not the stuff of fairy tales at all.

"Okay, okay." Turner sat up, swung his legs off the couch and stood. The dog got on shore with him, and the little monkey was still attached to his hand. Tessa pulled him through the swinging door into the kitchen. Harper sneaked in, too.

Turner stopped and suppressed a groan. "Wrong turn. North Pole."

It did indeed feel like Santa's workshop. A spicy aroma permeated the air. Christmas music was playing and the kitchen was a flurry of colorful activity. Cole, Emma, Rick, Andrea and Casey were all here. Each had on a Christmas apron, and they seemed to be on an assembly line of cookie production.

"I thought you guys would still be busy with the tree."

Cole looked up at him. "That was hours ago, buddy. You've been out like a light."

Turner contemplated that a little uneasily. He had slept, which was good, but so deeply? On a couch in the middle of a house full of people? What had happened to his soldier's gift for sleeping with one eye open?

It occurred to him something was changing. He was being plunged into the things he feared most: sleeping, Christmas, tears. It was like tossing a person who was terrified of water into a lake.

Sink or swim.

And he was swimming. He was not sinking. And it was because of her.

He glanced at Casey. Her cheeks were glowing and pink from being outside; her vigorously straightened hair was clipped back sternly for work in the kitchen. Little curls were escaping the clip, and she did that thing she did—blew them out of the way—without having any idea at all how sexy it was.

So he felt an increasing sense of safety, and about as unsafe as he had ever felt, at the very same time. His mission no longer felt clear. Oh, yes, that was definitely a headache of major proportions developing. He made himself look at something besides Casey.

Cole, high powered businessman, was working a food processor, his tongue caught between his teeth in fierce concentration. Rick, the fireman, was using the considerable strength in his arms to roll out sheets of dark, sugary looking dough.

The women were using cookie cutters, though

really, it felt as if, despite his efforts to look at everyone else, Turner could see only Casey, who was moving the freshly cut cookies onto baking sheets.

Gingerbread men, big surprise.

Her hair being pulled back so severely only served to show off the amazing height of her cheekbones, the tender curve of her neck.

"So, what woke you up?" Cole said, grinning at him. "I thought you were going to sleep for a week."

"I had a little nudge from my friend," Turner said, looking down. Tessa was still tugging on his hand, trying to get him to move along.

"Tess, I told you to leave him alone," Rick said sternly.

"I want him to make cookies with me," Tessa said, unrepentant. She let go of his hand, finally, and climbed up on a stool beside Andrea. Grabbing a cutter, the little girl began to press out cookies randomly from the sheet of dark dough.

"Are you ever making cookies," Turner said. He noticed Casey would not look at him, bent over those cookies as if they were one of her research projects.

So she, too, wanted to take a step back from the intensity of what had leaped up between them yesterday.

The sleep must have made some defenses come down, because when he saw her avoiding looking at him, it was achingly apparent to him he had hurt her all those years ago, so wrapped up in himself that the possibility she might have pined for him had never occurred to him.

He remembered that night so well. Fresh out of training, he'd known he was leaving on his first assignment. It was the first time he had experienced the predeployment intensity, a sense that he was about to embark on a mission that was highly dangerous and probably life threatening. It had given him a heightened awareness of being alive. Each breath had felt exquisite, each encounter lit from within.

And most especially that applied to his encounter with bridesmaid Casey. The few days they had spent together after the wedding had had an almost magical quality. Though they'd stopped well short of physical intimacy, Turner had never felt so alive or so connected to another human being.

Since then, he had experienced that predeployment high on many occasions. True, never quite as sweetly as that first time.

He studied Casey, and knew despite the fact she was a professional, a doctor, a research scientist, at her core was still that sweet, deep-thinking girl who had captivated him that night.

Could he make up for his insensitivity to her? Should he try?

Probably not. Yesterday, playing in the snow with

her, should have been a lesson to him. He might not be able to control where the fire went once it started burning.

Besides, it would ask him to be something he was not. His brothers perceived him as colossally insensitive and self-centered, and he had no proof that they were wrong.

Leave that girl alone, he ordered himself.

He had his own wounds to nurse, his own demons to battle, his own hard choices that needed to be made.

But standing here in this kitchen, with good smells all around him, feeling safe, surrounded by people who were cheerful and uncomplicated, he had a sudden memory.

A long time ago, back when the world had worked the way it was supposed to, his dad had shown him over and over what it was to be a good man.

When he was twelve, Turner hadn't made the rep team for hockey that year. He'd been sulking and stewing, breaking things, snapping at his mother and his brothers a whole two weeks after the cut, which was probably a week after he should have been over it.

His dad, without explanation, had ordered him into the car one Saturday morning. Without a word he had driven him to the children's hospital in a neighboring community. Still without a word, his father had gathered packages from the trunk, handing some to Turner to carry.

Once inside it had become clear to Turner, that this was not his dad's first visit. He knew some of the kids by name. He had books and small gifts tucked into his pockets, puzzles and coloring books and NERF toys in the packages.

He'd introduced Turner as a hockey player, and little boys who would never skate plied him with questions loaded with curiosity and envy.

"Do you get it, son?" his dad had asked him as they drove home.

"Yeah, I do." He got it. That he lived a privileged life. That he was fortunate to be able to lace up skates and take to the ice.

His dad hadn't said a word, just reached across and rested his hand on his shoulder, leaving it there for the rest of the trip home.

But Turner realized, since the death of his father, that his life had not felt quite so privileged. He was not always surrounded by good fortune and luck. He had experienced loss.

What would his father have thought if Turner used that as an excuse not to be a good man? His dad had been a good man. Genuinely, and to the core. He hadn't been good because he needed the approval of others, or to be showy. Being good had come as naturally to him as breathing. Once, Turner had aspired to be just like him. Now?

Was there anything left in him that could be?

Wasn't that what he was here to find out, as he stood at this crossroad, wondering which road to take?

He moseyed up to Casey, saw that she planned to act cool, but then she did a double take.

"What's wrong?" she asked.

"What do you mean, what's wrong?" He didn't like being read. He thought he probably sounded defensive.

"You look like you have a headache."

"I do," he admitted, mulling over how he had been able to keep his vulnerabilities successfully to himself for a long, long time. "Shouldn't have fallen asleep during the day."

"You want something for it?"

Just like he was not used to children and dogs, he was not used to this. Tenderness.

"I'll suck it up." To prove he was strong, not weak.

"Very manly," she said, with a roll of her eyes.

"You know what you look like with your hair like that?" he said, anxious, suddenly, to get her to stop gazing at him with that expression that made him want soft things—a shoulder to put his head on, a soothing hand on his brow.

It worked. She looked wary instead of compassionate. Wariness he could handle.

"Olive Oyl."

"Olive oil?" she said, puzzled.

"Popeye's girlfriend."

"Just because you kissed me yesterday," Casey whispered, casting a glance around her, "don't get any ideas about me being your girlfriend."

Oh, yeah, he had done an imitation of Popeye!

"I kissed you?" he sputtered in an undertone. "You started that! And don't worry. I don't have any ideas about you being my girlfriend."

Even though she'd said it first, now she looked slightly wounded.

Sorry, Dad. Turner's attempt to be a good man had lasted about fifteen seconds. "Not that that's about you," he said hastily, under his breath.

"Thanks, you educated me about the nature of cads and my good fortune around them yesterday," she hissed back.

"Look, it's not about you. I don't do attachment. That's my favor to the world. And you."

She looked perplexed. "What?"

Stop talking, he ordered himself. "I do the kind of work where people come home in bags," he said quietly, for her ears only. "It's not fair to let people love you when you take those kinds of risks."

And he knew. Burned into him, as badly as Ken's blood, were the sobs of the man's wife, the cries of his children.

Turner braced himself. Casey had a perfect opportunity to say she would never love him, anyway. That he had nothing to worry about in that department, at all.

Instead, she did what he least expected.

She reached up and cupped her hand tenderly along his jawline. She looked at him so softly it felt as if his armor was melting.

"Oh, Turner," she said, as if her heart were breaking for him. "Oh, Turner. Now I see what it is about you that children and dogs love."

She glanced at the ever faithful Harper, and kept her hand on his cheek, oblivious to the other occupants of the room.

"That's ridiculous. I probably smell like a hamburger."

"You don't," she said, and then blushed and took her hand away. He thought she would look around to see if anyone had noticed, but she didn't. She didn't seem at all perturbed that she might have been caught in that easily misinterpreted act of pure tenderness.

Turner felt as if his very survival depended on backtracking, on lightening things up between them. "Hey, I thought that was Harper sniffing my neck while I was sleeping on the couch."

Then Casey blushed *and* smiled. That was a knockout combination.

"Come on," she said. "You showed me how to make snowmen. I'll show you how to make gingerbread men."

He had the perfect excuse to beg off. He had a headache.

Had had a headache. Her touch seemed to have erased it. Was that even possible?

It seemed to Turner that the thing called *love*—the thing he had most tried to avoid, that he had denied needing at every turn—was right here in the kitchen.

With these people that were his friends.

In the uncomplicated affection of a dog. And a child.

In Casey's angel-soft touch against the whisker-roughened surface of his cheek.

It was what he had been running from since the day his father had died. It was what had failed him, and what he had failed, too. He wanted to run from what suddenly seemed to him to be an invitation he did not want to accept.

Turner had complete confidence in himself as a courageous man. He had stood beside buddies in shadowy battles, had stood his ground when others would have run, had said yes a thousand times when other men would have said no.

But now he understood he had only scraped the surface of the meaning of courage.

Suddenly, he couldn't have left the kitchen if he wanted to. He needed to be here. He needed to be here if there was any hope at all for him to ever be the man his father had hoped he would become.

CHAPTER TWELVE

"How was the hunt for the perfect tree? Hokey?"

Casey knew something had just happened. Something unexpected. And important. Turner had told her things about himself that bordered on sacred.

He had set an impossible mission for himself. To protect the whole world from the pain of loving him.

It was heartbreakingly honorable, and if she ever said such a thing to him, she knew he would run for the door.

Even now, his staying here seemed tenuous.

She had to give him room. She had to let him breathe.

And she had to—in the spirit of Christmas, if nothing else—give him a gift. A break from the self-imposed loneliness he wore around himself like an invisible cloak. She had to become the kind of person she wanted the mother of her child to be.

She had known why he hadn't come on the outing for the tree this morning. He hadn't come so that she would go.

Now she felt ashamed that she had been so deeply relieved when he'd bowed out so that she could be more comfortable.

Casey vowed she would not let that happen again.

"It was such good fun," she said with a sigh, regretting that he had not been there. "Did your family do things like that when you were growing up? You and your brothers?"

Somehow, she felt she wanted to reconnect him to what he had lost over the years.

"Sure, we'd go get a tree from the woods. Did they let you touch the ax?"

So, he was as determined not to go there as she was to take him.

"Are you trying to start an argument?"

"What makes you say that?"

"Because you're insinuating I'm incompetent with an ax!"

"They did let you touch it!"

"You're trying to start an argument because you don't want me to delve into the rift between you and your brothers."

He looked at her long and hard. "We have to discuss the terms of that truce."

"We called off the truce."

"Can we just bake cookies then?"

"Ah," she said, knowing it was time to back off. "If I'm not mistaken, you are begging to bake cookies."

"You know something, Casey? You are way too smart for your own good."

"I know," she said, and despite the fact no truce had been agreed on, they settled into the task at hand like two people who had figured out there might be some advantages to being a team.

"Where would you place gingerbread men on the hokey scale?" he asked her.

She glanced up at him. Did his eyes linger on her lips before she looked swiftly away? "Somewhere between snowmen and Christmas trees," she said.

"How come so many cookies?"

"We're going to give them out as guest gifts at the vow renewal. So we're making some gingerbread grooms and some gingerbread brides. And we thought we'd make a few extras, to donate to the Barrow's Cove Food Bank. To help fill the Christmas hampers."

"Whose idea was that?" he asked.

Casey shrugged uncomfortably.

"Yours," he said. Casey was a woman his father would have approved of.

Turner felt the oddest tug of emotion at this humble effort to make the world a better place, one cookie at a time.

It was like her hand on his cheek, and her eyes, soft, on his face.

Small things.

Almost inconsequential.

It occurred to him such gestures of small kindnesses were probably far more powerful in bringing about real change than all the men who marched off to war, set on making all that was wrong in the world right.

Casey picked that moment to glance up at him.

That night all those years ago, he had thought her dark eyes saw him in a way no one else ever had.

And despite many predeployment nights since then, it occurred to him he had never experienced *that* again.

"How many cookies?" he asked.

"We thought half a dozen cookies per hamper, and then two for each guest, so…" she closed her eyes for a moment "…about four hundred cookies."

"Wow," Emily said, overhearing, and looking at her friend with affection and awe. "How do you do that? Math in your head. And so fast!"

Casey shrugged uncomfortably. "Born geek," she muttered, and shot Turner a look.

But he didn't see a geek. He saw a woman who was brilliant. And beautiful. And trying hard not to be vulnerable.

Could he be a good man, without causing more harm than good? Did he have a choice? He was here. She was here.

"What do you want me to do?" he asked gruffly.

"Those ones on the counter are ready for decorating. Why don't you and Tessa start icing them?"

"That sounds a little too delicate for me." There were a lot of things in this room that were way too delicate for a man who had killed people for a living. "How about if I start on the dishes?"

But neither of these females was interested in the agenda that would be safest for him.

"No," Tessa said imperiously. "You help me."

"Tessa," Rick said sternly. "Quit being so bossy."

The little girl's face crumpled. Her eyes clenched shut.

"Geez, don't do that!" Turner said. "I'll help you."

The grimace dissolved into a smile.

"Sorry," Rick said. "She has a little issue with being in control."

"It's okay."

"I want you to help, too," Tessa said, tugging on Casey's sleeve.

With the little girl on a stool between them, they took cooled cookies off the pans and laid out row after row of gingerbread men and women.

Andrea popped several full bags of icing in front of them, and one of candy-coated chocolate buttons. "Casey, why don't you and Turner do the faces? Tess can do the buttons."

"No eating the buttons," Turner warned Tessa, and she giggled.

"You're silly," she decided.

"Watch who you're calling silly," he groused, and was rewarded when both she and Casey giggled. "You must call me Master Icer."

He squeezed some icing out of a bag onto the head of a gingerbread man.

"He looks like a monster," Tessa howled, disparaging of Turner's artistic skill.

"Well," he said, "it really doesn't matter. You know why?"

She shook her head.

"Because this is the test cookie. I'm eating it."

He broke the cookie into three pieces, then contemplated them solemnly. "I'm the biggest and the master icer, so I get the biggest piece." He popped the whole chunk into his mouth, then handed Tessa a piece and Casey another.

"You're going to ruin our dinner," Casey protested.

"Oh, boy. Haven't you heard of happy hour? It's time for cookies somewhere, isn't it, princess?"

"Yeah," Tessa said, beaming at him for recognizing her as a princess. "Yum."

"You know what it tastes like?"

"What?"

"Like we should have another one."

Tessa broke into a fit of giggles.

"Master Icer?" Casey said a trace sardonically,

"We have four hundred cookies to decorate, so you're going to have to pick up the pace a bit."

He ate faster.

Even Casey laughed, taking in Tessa's delight. "See?" she said. "Kids and dogs."

He realized he felt happy to make her laugh. Happy for this simple moment of changing the world in a simple way, one cookie at a time, one smile at a time, one laugh at a time.

It occurred to him that, for a few minutes, anyway, he had left his baggage behind. And he had fit into this wholesome world just fine.

And liked being here, too.

Turner wondered if that meant he had just moved closer to making the decision he'd come here to ponder.

He and Casey began to put piped, white icing faces on the cookies. Tongue caught between her teeth in concentration, she did the girls, making exaggerated eyelashes and lips for them, while he did the boys. Tessa did buttons.

They all stared at the first completed row of cookies with just a little bit of awe. They looked terrific!

"What would you give this on the hokey scale?" he muttered to Casey.

"Would the hokey scale be out of ten?" she asked.

"Sure."

"How about an eleven?"

"Sixteen."

"One hundred and two," Tessa crowed, determined not to be left out of the conversation.

And then they laughed. It was a small thing, that shared laugh, and yet it felt surprisingly good. Much like Turner had felt yesterday, when they'd built the snowmen. He allowed himself to sink into it.

Sink into the simple pleasure of sharing this warm, fragrant kitchen with friends on a snowy day, trying to make Christmas just a little better for someone else.

He glanced at Casey's shining face.

And was pretty sure he didn't mean the food bank clients, either.

Casey looked at Turner's dark head bent close to Tessa's as he put an icing smile on a gingerbread groom. The little girl waited with the "special" buttons, silver for the vow-renewal cookies.

Despite claiming discomfort, he seemed very at ease with the child. He would be a natural as a daddy, and Casey wondered why he wasn't.

And then told herself, and sternly, too, that was none of her business.

The last two days—building snowmen, everyone pitching in to cook dinners and clean up after, going out in search of a perfect tree—were what she had always hoped for around Christmas as a child. She had dreamed of the kind of days she read about in books and saw in movies, days filled with laughter and fun and a sense of connection with other people.

This was the life she wanted for her own child. It was no surprise to her that she would feel it here. The only times she had ever come close to feeling this way before had always been here, at the Gingerbread Inn.

And in spite of her family, not because of them. The Gingerbread Girls had always given her this gift—creating a sense of the family she wanted and did not have.

She could see Turner had had it, too.

And lost it somehow.

In the very spirit of the Christmas she wanted to believe in for her own child, Casey was determined to help him get it back. Whether he wanted her help or not.

She slid a look at him. He radiated self-certainty and self-reliance. He would not want any help from her.

And that was not going to stop her.

Tonight, she was going to get on her computer and track his brothers down. She looked at his face, open now as he leaned over cookies with Tessa.

Casey had the feeling she might be going where angels feared to tread.

Hours later, she closed her computer and rubbed

her eyes. She had found both Turner's brothers on Facebook and sent them a message. I am a friend of Turner's. I need to talk to you. She had hesitated just a second, and then added, URGENT.

She had felt so sure she was doing the right thing, but now, uncertainty hit her. She wasn't even able to repair her own relationship with her mother. What made Casey think she knew what was best for him?

She reminded herself it was only a message. She hadn't actually done anything yet.

She glanced at her bedside clock. Ten at night. She didn't feel tired. She went to her window and looked out, wondering if she might see Turner skating. It was a beautiful night, with a full moon painting the amazing snow-filled world in luminescent shades of silver.

If he was out there, would she join him?

She was aware, as she went to the window, that she was hoping he would be.

What she saw was him heading along the shore of the lake, the dog beside him. Casey hesitated only a moment before grabbing her coat and racing out the door after him.

He sensed her coming and turned, waited for her.

"Where are you going?"

"Just for a walk." After the slightest hesitation, he added, "Do you want to come?"

"Yes."

The silence was companionable, the dog racing

ahead and then back. A snowmobile had been by, making a nice, hard-packed trail that was comfortable for two people to walk on side by side.

They passed cabins boarded up for the winter, crossed a little footbridge that spanned a small creek, fast running and deep enough to be not quite frozen despite the frigid nights. They stopped in the middle of the bridge, gazed down at the water, listened to it tinkle over shards of ice.

Casey had never walked at night in the snow. It was a quiet she had never experienced before. When she slipped slightly, Turner took her hand, and even after she had found her footing, he didn't let go.

Harper was sniffing around the foundation of one of the cabins. Suddenly, she broke the silence of the night and began to bark.

"Hey, that's enough," Turner said.

But the dog was now racing back and forth, barking frantically, trying to dig her way under the lattice.

Turner let go of Casey's hand and went to retrieve the dog. But just as he got close, a raccoon shot from under the cabin, the dog hot on its heels.

In seconds they were both on the lake, and then the worst possible thing happened.

The ice, thin there at the mouth of the creek, gave an ominous crack. While the raccoon skittered away, Harper screeched to a halt, stared with doggie consternation at the spiderweb of cracks shooting out around her feet. And then the ice broke and the beautiful dog plunged into the water.

CHAPTER THIRTEEN

CASEY DIDN'T EVEN think. She ran toward the dog, which was paddling frantically in the icy water. Harper was trying to heave herself up onto the ice, but succeeded only in breaking it more. Casey could see the panic on the poor creature's face.

"No! Casey! No!"

She could hear a terrible urgency in Turner's voice, could see him running toward her as if he intended to tackle her. But she felt the same urgency to get to Harper as he felt to get to her. She took advantage of the distance between them and put on a burst of speed.

"Casey, don't!"

She was on the ice now. She could nearly reach Harper. Casey could feel the ice giving, as if it had a faint spring to it like a trampoline. She recognized, suddenly, that she hadn't thought this through. But she was so close!

Some snippet of knowledge about ice penetrated her adrenaline-infused state. She flopped onto her belly, crawled the remaining few feet, dispersing her weight over the fragile surface. The dog, relief in every wrinkle of her loving features, swam to her. Casey reached out for her paws.

Harper flailed and the ice broke.

It was a slow process, like a mirror shattering. First a spiderweb of cracks, then a groan as the ice settled.

Casey tried to wriggle backward but it was too late. Frigid water raced up onto the sinking slab. Then the ice shelf gave way and she plunged into the lake.

The shock of the cold hit her like a sledgehammer as the water closed over her. Somehow, she got her head clear and was able to turn and grab at the ledge of ice. Her breath was coming in great gasping gulps.

Somehow, Turner's voice penetrated her panic.

Don't come, she thought, the silent scream rising above the sheer panic that was enveloping her. It occurred to her he *would* come. That nothing would stop him. And that nobody knew where they were and that they were all going to die out here.

"Listen to me."

His voice was like a life rope, and she turned her full attention toward it. "You have to steady your breath. You are hyperventilating. You are experiencing cold shock. You cannot die from it. Do you hear me?"

Did she nod? She wasn't sure.

"That's better," he said, as she struggled to stop gasping for air, to draw in slower breaths. How could she be so cold and *still* respond to the praise in his voice?

"Casey, you need to get your elbows up on the ice and see if you can pull yourself out of the water, even a bit. Use your legs. Kick as if you are swimming. Casey, do it! I know you can do it."

The firm calm in his voice reached her and she responded to it. Somehow, she found the strength to get one elbow up on the ice. It broke away.

"Kick. Try again."

This time she was able to haul herself up. The ice, miraculously, held.

"Breathe. Listen to me. Breathe in slowly as I count to three. One. Two. Three. Breathe out slowly as I count to three."

The dog had been swimming in frantic circles. Now she came up behind her.

If Harper started to scramble up on her in a panic, it occurred to Casey's shocked mind, they were both going to die.

But Harper put her paws on Casey's shoulders, wriggled up against her and gently clung. They both hung there on a precipice between life and death.

But Casey knew Turner was not going to let them die.

"Keep breathing," he said. His voice was the life

rope, calm, assured. "One. Two. Three. Don't try to pull yourself out. Your clothes are going to be too heavy to get yourself out. Keep counting."

And then, to her dismay, instead of coming for her, he turned and ran away from the water's edge.

It seemed like forever before he returned. When he did, he had a ladder. He laid it on the ice, shoved it out to her. She grabbed for it, caught it, held on for dear life. But when she tried to pull herself up on it, she could see he had been right.

Her saturated clothes were way too heavy and the strength had been sapped from her limbs by the excruciating cold.

"I just want you to look at me. Nothing else."

Her eyes locked on his, and though she was so cold, and still partway in the water, it was as if the rescue was complete already.

She knew, with a soul-deep kind of knowing, that in a matter of minutes this would all be over. He was going to save her. He did not have a single doubt, and that confidence ran the length of the ladder to her. It lifted her spirits to a place where she could hang on.

He began to crawl along the ladder toward her. The ice creaked ominously as he crept forward. Once, it cracked loudly and he stopped. But having evaluated that the ladder was distributing his weight across a large surface of the ice, he moved forward again.

Finally, he reached her. He grabbed her wrists and began to scoot backward.

"Just keep watching my face," he said. "Don't look at anything else, don't think about anything else. It's just like skating."

Of course, it was the furthest thing from that magical experience she had had, skating with him, but somehow his invoking that memory was a good thing. He had her. He had her then, and he had her now.

"Kick your legs," he told her. "Kick as hard as you can."

She did exactly as he ordered. She watched his face. She was soothed by the calm in it, by the grim determination.

A man less strong, she knew, would not have been able to do what he was doing. He was literally hauling her out of the water onto the ice. At first it broke away under her weight. She was afraid the ladder would go in, and him with it, but he just waited it out, scooted back, his hands bands of iron around her wrists. When he had her more out of the water than in, he yanked the dog off her shoulders and literally tossed Harper onto more stable ice.

Then he flipped Casey over, sat up, wrapped his legs around her torso and crab-walked backward, dragging her with him.

And somehow she knew this was what he did. And he did it well. He dealt in life-and-death crises. She suspected he did it all the time. How else could he do it as naturally as breathing?

"Don't even try it," he warned when she attempted, groggily, to get her feet under her. Her mind was not working correctly. Everything was in slow motion.

The dog got on shore, shook herself weakly. Casey took her eyes from his only for a second to watch Harper find solid ground on the embankment and lie down, unmoving.

Turner pulled her backward until they were at the last rung of the ladder. And then he stood up.

The ice groaned.

Panic tried to rear up in her, but he was straddling the ladder, still distributing his weight.

He lifted her, slung her over his shoulder like a sack of potatoes, and ran. The ice snapped and cracked behind them.

And then they, too, were on the shore.

It occurred to her it was not over. She was wet and frozen. How far had they walked? As much as a mile?

"C-could I f-f-freeze to d-death still?" The words took effort, way too much effort.

"Not on my watch," he said, and again his confidence and his competence transferred directly to her. But would that be enough to keep her going until he got them back to the inn?

He was not going back to the inn. He hit the

embankment running, not deterred by her extra weight at all. He ran to the cabin, shifted her limp form on his shoulder, and booted the door. With the second kick the wood splintered, and with the third the door crashed open.

She lifted her head. The dog was still lying as if dead, by the shore of the lake.

"H-Harper," she called weakly.

"Forget the damned dog. You nearly died for her."

They were in the cabin's main room. Turner went down on one knee, slid her off his shoulder onto a worn couch. He moved quickly away from her, went through another door, came back with blankets ripped from a bed.

If she had hoped for warmth in the cabin, she was dead wrong. It seemed colder than outside. She had never been so cold. Her body was so numb it was beyond pain.

Wordlessly, working precisely, he began to strip her sopping clothes from her. First her jacket, then her boots.

He grabbed the hem of her sweater, pulled it off her wooden, uncooperative limbs and over her head. It tangled briefly in her hair, and when he tugged it free with urgency, she felt almost thankful to feel the pain of her hair being pulled. To feel anything.

His hands went to her blouse.

"Oh, no," she managed to whisper, mortified. "Don't."

"Get real. Death or modesty. Guess which one is out the window?"

He didn't undo the buttons on her shirt, just yanked, hard, and they all popped free and rattled across the wooden floor.

He tried to peel the sleeves off, but her limbs were not working now, like funny floppy things in no way connected to her. He had to manipulate them, struggling to get the sopping clothes off her pebbled, frozen flesh.

At another time, she might have been more self-conscious, but her brain was feeling sluggish, still moving in slow motion.

This was not the time to be wondering what she had put on for underwear this morning, but wonder she did.

Still, when his hands found the clasp at the back of her bra—and very expertly at that—nothing changed in the professional, cool cast of his face. His expression showed nothing except determination as he pulled apart the clasp and dropped her bra to the floor.

He shoved her down, unsnapped her jeans, peeled them over her hips, down her thighs and off.

He reached for her panties.

"Don't," she rasped. She didn't have the strength to push his hands away.

"Sorry," he said, not very sincerely. The panties were gone.

She barely had time to contemplate her nakedness before Turner had her wrapped in coarse blankets, tight as a sausage in a roll.

"P-p-please. The d-d-dog."

He gave her an exasperated look. She began to cry.

Without another word he went out the door and came back with Harper, dumped her unceremoniously in front of a cold hearth. Casey noticed the front of Turner's coat was soaked, too.

"Th-thank you." She meant for getting the dog, but she was too exhausted to elaborate. It didn't matter. Turner didn't acknowledge her.

Working quickly, his manner methodical and thorough, he crumpled paper and reached for kindling, both from a wood box next to the fireplace. He set them carefully, played around with the damper and then lit a match, also taken from the box. He got down on his knees, blowing gently, reminding her of the time he had blown on her cold hands.

Turner. Turner Kennedy. Bringing warmth to a world gone cold. In so many, many different ways.

He watched carefully for the first lick of flames, and only when fire crackled along the kindling did he start adding wood. And then more.

When that was done, he went and hauled a mattress out of the bedroom, laid it right in front of the fire. And then he disappeared and came back with a towel from somewhere. He sat her up in her blanket strait jacket and rubbed her hair hard with the towel.

"Ouch."

"Hey, suck it up. Compared to what I'd like to do to you, you're getting off easy." He continued toweling her hair, squeezing the extra water out of it, toweling some more.

"What?"

"I told you not to go out after the dog," he said sternly. "What the hell is the matter with you?"

"What would you like to do to me?" she whispered.

"Strangulation comes to mind." But his eyes moved to her lips, and then away. It seemed to her he was extra rough with the towel then.

"Don't be mad." Her chattering teeth made the words sound strangled.

"Yeah, why be mad? You could have got yourself killed over a stupid dog—"

"She's worth it," Casey said stubbornly.

He groaned. "And I've been dying to get my hands in your hair and here we are. Of course, it's not exactly what I expected, but then is anything ever, around you? And it wasn't worth it. No dog is worth a human life."

"I put you in danger, too," she said mournfully. "I'm sorry."

"Not sorry about putting yourself in danger, but sorry about putting me in danger." He snorted with disgust. "You're the one who is going to cure cancer. You're worth ten of me, Casey."

"I am not," she said softly.

"Yeah, well, we'll open the debate later." He tossed down the towel, lifted her easily into his arms, strode across the room with her and set her down on the mattress with a gentleness that belied the sternness in his tone.

"I-I'm not w-w-warming up."

His tone changed completely. "I know, sweetheart. Hang in there."

Sweetheart.

If only all these circumstances were different. To be in a cabin with him, in nothing more than a blanket, and to have him call her sweetheart.

Not like that, though. Not like a person speaking to a child who needed to be comforted.

In the same methodical way that he had rid her of her clothing, Turner began to strip off his own clothes. He tossed off his jacket, wet from the rescue and her hair. His hands flew down the buttons of his shirt, and he yanked it open, revealing the utter perfection of his chest, painted in the golden glow of the strengthening fire.

"Is it normal to feel drunk?" she whispered.

"Yeah, all the girls feel that way when I take off my shirt," he said sardonically.

And he didn't stop at just his shirt, either!

Casey could feel her eyes going round with wonder as his hands went to the snap on his jeans, opened it, and then the zipper. He shrugged out of the pants, stepped from the puddle of denim on the floor.

His fingers found the waistband of his underwear, and through her chattering teeth she gasped.

He hesitated then, for the first time since this whole debacle had started. He stared at her, disconcerted, as if so far he had managed to think of her just as an exercise in survival. After a second, his hands moved away from the band, and the underwear stayed.

Her mind slowed from the cold, Casey couldn't figure out if she was very, very relieved or very, very disappointed.

And then he crouched beside her, tugged up the corner of the blanket and slipped onto the mattress beside her.

"Sorry, babe, it's the best way I know to get some warmth into you. Transfer my body heat. Slow enough not to do harm. Quick enough to prevent hypothermia."

He wrapped his arms around her and pulled her in close.

Her mind processed the information.

Turner Kennedy and I are wrapped in a blanket together. All that is preventing us from total nakedness is the thin fabric of his shorts.

The sad part? The surface of her skin was so cold it was without sensation. He might as well have been a frozen fish.

CHAPTER FOURTEEN

TURNER TUCKED THE blankets around them as tightly as he could, and then put his arms around her again, pulling her more closely to him.

The dog whined, and came and lay against his back.

The fire crackled on the other side of him.

"I like your shorts," she decided, and then realized she had said it out loud. "I mean, they're not Jockeys and not boxers. What are they?"

He swore softly and was silent.

"There's got to be a name for that." She giggled. "Not tighty whities, but—"

"Would you stop it?"

"I would, honestly, but I don't think I can. Tighty mighties?"

"Casey, I'm begging you. Stop."

"Just tell me the name."

"If I tell you, you'll never mention it again, ever?"

"I promise."

"Boxer briefs."

"Oh," she said, and then sighed. "I really like them. Were mine okay?"

"Your what?" he asked in a strangled tone.

"My undies. I really wasn't expecting anyone to see them today."

"I didn't really notice."

"Please tell me I was not wearing the full coverage ones that have the days of the week on them."

"You're killing me here."

"Sunday is pink," she prompted.

"Okay. It was not Sunday. Or full coverage."

"So, you did look!"

"Casey, I'm a man. I looked. Not the red lacy ones. White. Bikini."

She felt inordinately pleased that for some reason she had not chosen her practical underwear this morning. Her new leaf was really going all to hell when she thought about it.

But she didn't feel like thinking about it right now!

"You said you didn't notice."

"You caught me then. I was lying. It was one of those self-preserving kinds of lies a man tells when he can't possibly win. Because if I looked—and worse, noticed—I'd be some kind of pervert. And if I didn't notice, then you might think you didn't measure up."

"Did I? Measure up?"

"I'm trying to be professional here."

She pondered that. "Professional what? What kind of government contracts did you say you do?"

"I didn't say."

"Sensitive work," she remembered. "You save people, don't you?"

He snorted. "I'm no hero, Casey. Don't even think it. You have started down the road of disillusionment."

"How can I not think it, when you saved me?" she whispered, suddenly feeling very sober. "Turner, you saved my life. How did you know? How do you know how to do all these things?"

"It's no big deal," he said, and he meant it. "That's what I get paid for. To keep a clear head when all hell is breaking loose."

"You're amazing."

"If I was that amazing, I wouldn't have left home without a cell phone," he said ruefully.

"No," she said. "Turner, you are the most amazing man I've ever met. And that was before I saw you in your boxer shorts. Boxer briefs."

"Yeah, well, survivor's euphoria."

"Is that why I feel like giggling?"

"Unless that's me in my boxer briefs again, yeah, probably."

"Euphoria," she whispered, contemplating it, liking the way the word rolled through her mind like warm mist. And that was exactly what she felt lying there, thawing out, wrapped tightly in a blanket, his naked body sharing his warmth with her. Absolute and utter euphoria, as if she had never had a better moment in her entire life.

"I should be mortified," she said out loud. Were her words slurring slightly, as if she was drunk? "But I'm not. I'm euphoric. And at least I'm not wearing the pink ones that say Sunday on them. Are you euphoric, too, Turner?"

"Oh, sure," he said gruffly, "I'm naked with a beautiful woman under the worst possible circumstances. You have pried personal information from me about my underwear and yours. But as I said before, I have a feeling nothing with you ever goes as expected, does it?"

"Why? Were you expecting this? Were you expecting us to be naked together? Sometime?"

He groaned. "My only defense is a weak one, and I'm falling back on it, even though I've already used it. I'm a man. Men think like that."

"Wow," she said, feeling as if he had announced the discovery of a new planet. "Men think naked thoughts. All the time?"

"Just about," he said.

"With everybody?" She giggled. "Every body— get it?"

"No," he said gruffly, "not with every body."

"So, if you had to get naked with someone to

keep them from dying, would you be pretty glad it was me?"

"Casey?"

"Hmm?"

"Quit talking now. I'm begging you."

"If you just answer that one question, I promise I will."

But he didn't answer. He tucked her in even closer, put his chin on top of her head and let her bury her face in his chest.

And it felt like an answer, even if it didn't have words.

The exhaustion had caught up to her. She was sleeping. Cuddled to him as she was, Casey's shivering was beginning to become less violent, her body beginning, just beginning, to feel less like a block of ice. Turner knew that meant they were coming out of the danger zone.

He was keeping his body between her and the fire now. His body heat would warm her up at a good rate; the fire might do it too quickly.

Out of the danger zone? They were lying naked in each other arms, and they had just had a rather intimate discussion about underthings.

So, possibly they were entering a danger zone of a whole other kind, not that he would ever take advantage of what she was feeling.

Gratitude. Relief. Euphoria.

It was probably as close as she had ever come

to a near-death experience. He had brushes with them all the time.

But there was a difference here, and he pondered that.

In all those other situations, it had been a mission. Everything rehearsed and controlled, as much as it was humanly possible to do. He knew what he was getting into, what tools and skills he would use, what he could control and what he could not.

He left nothing to that most precarious of things, chance.

Turner believed in himself, and the people he was surrounded with. He believed in carefully calculated odds, even though those odds were not always in his favor.

What he did not believe in was miracles.

And yet, when he looked at what had happened tonight out there on the broken ice, it had the markings of the miraculous. What were the chances that a ladder would be leaning up against the cabin? What were the chances that there would *be* a cabin? Full of every single thing he needed to keep her alive?

What if she'd been out here walking by herself?

A miracle, he thought, and pondered that. Maybe he was experiencing a bit of euphoria, after all.

Turner waited another hour, and then two, feeling warmth sliding back into her body before he finally released her and moved away. The dog protested and Casey mewed in her sleep, but he tucked the blankets tight around her.

Harper, still very wet, was going to try and snuggle into Casey, so he found more towels and dried the dog off.

"Stupid mutt," he said.

Harper kissed him lavishly. Turner went and found an extra blanket, wrapped it around the dog.

Then he got Casey's frozen clothes from the floor by the couch. He took them outside, barely noticing the cold, and wrung them out.

They were not going to be ready for her to put back on in the morning.

Next he rummaged through the cupboards, coming up with broth and crackers. He found a pot. The propane for the stove had been turned off, so he stepped outside, found the tank valve and turned it on.

In moments the soup was bubbling briskly.

He ate some, then against his better judgment got a bowl and spoon-fed some to the dog.

He could go now, and get help.

But just then Casey cried out in her sleep, woke with a start, screaming, and scrabbled out from under the blankets.

He went to her instantly, pulled back the covers, crawled back in beside her, and held her tight. Her tears soaked his chest. He kissed the top of her head, and that seemed to finally settle her down.

"I dreamed I was back in the water," she said.

"It was just a dream. You're safe. Do you want something to eat? I made soup."

"I could have got us all killed," she said. "Instead of a celebration of love, poor Emily and Cole. More tragedy—

"Hey, don't even go there. That's not what happened."

"I could have killed you. One mistake, and you would have been dead. All of us out floating in the water."

"Stop it," he said sternly.

"I-I c-c-can't. So stupid. I'm st-stupid."

"It was an accident. Shit happens. Shhh, you're not stupid. You're about the furthest thing there is from stupid."

"Why couldn't I see? The dog went through the ice! Why did I just charge out there like that? Like an idiot."

"Because, for once," he said softly, "you were thinking with your heart instead of your head."

"That figures," she said. "That just bloody well figures. That's always when I get in trouble."

"Tell me about it," he said. "You tell me all about that, Casey."

Under normal circumstances she would have never told Turner Kennedy about the faulty radar of her heart.

But this wasn't normal.

Nothing about tonight felt normal.

Least of all what she was feeling for Turner. A trust as deep as anything she had ever felt.

"It's a long story if I start at the beginning," she said.

"We've got nothing but time."

"My dad could not be faithful to my mom," she said tentatively, because she knew that really was the beginning. "Some people say it's the nature of Italian men, but I don't think that was it."

She stopped. Heavens, was she really going to get into this? They were naked together, and she was going to discuss her childhood?

No, she was going to discuss the problem of thinking with her heart.

And that was better than the alternative, which she suspected was why he was encouraging her. He wanted her to think about *anything* except that water closing over her head, how close she had come to killing them.

And she wanted to think of anything except how strangely right it felt to be cuddled up in a blanket with a very nearly naked man.

"What do you think it was?" he asked, encouraging her.

"It was my brother getting cancer. I think my dad was unmanned by that. As if he should have been able to save him and protect him, and he couldn't."

"I think every man feels that way," Turner said

softly. "As if it is his highest calling to protect what is his."

His voice embraced her, accepted her, encouraged her to go on. But more, she had a feeling Turner Kennedy had just told her who he was.

"Go on," he said, his voice soft in the night, the crackling fire and his nearness lulling her into a place where she wanted to share confidences.

"And then when my brother died, my dad saw that as his greatest failure as a man. He couldn't face it. He kept the pain at bay by having affair after affair after affair. Each one an attempt to get his manhood back. That's my memory of my dad. Even here at the Gingerbread Inn. He was always flirting with my girlfriends' moms."

"You were embarrassed by him," Turner guessed gruffly.

"Oh, yes, but oddly, I was more embarrassed by my mom. She always knew what he was up to. She'd shriek and cry and throw things, but any real action? No. Why did she tolerate that? Why didn't she leave him?"

"It sounds almost as if you've forgiven your dad, but not your mom."

"It's easier to forgive deceased people."

"What's going on with your mom, Casey? How come you aren't spending Christmas with her?"

"How do you know I'm not?"

"Emily told me. She said when she and Cole

planned this, they wanted everybody to be able to get home after their ceremony and have Christmas with their families. So, how come you aren't?"

Casey contemplated the fact that Emily had said anything to him about her, but then gave in to the temptation to share it. She said quietly, "Can you keep a secret, Turner?"

"Oh, yeah. That's my life. Keeping secrets."

"When he died, my mom joined a convent. When I asked her to spend Christmas with me, it was no, she was serving Christmas dinner to the poor. But I was welcome to join her. As long as I remember she's Sister Maria Celeste now, and not Mom. She seems much happier being that than she ever was being my mother."

"Oh, boy," he said, his voice a low growl of sympathy. "So there it is, finally. Why you're sensitive to the topic of nuns right now. I'm sorry, Casey."

"I don't want you to feel sorry for me!"

"How can I not? Your life has just been one abandonment after another, hasn't it? Even me, leaving you the way I did."

"Why *did* you leave me like that? Without even a goodbye?"

"Men are jerks. Topped off with the jerk you got engaged to."

"You're not like him, but that's what I mean about following my heart," she said sadly. "How did it lead me right to my father? How could I be so stupid as to pick Sebastian out across a crowded room—or a crowded lab, as it was? How could I be so stupid as to fall in love with a man who was going to be unfaithful? Just like my dad."

"You wanted somebody to love you, Casey. There is nothing wrong with that."

"Yes," she said sadly. "It's that clear to you, isn't it? I was just desperate for someone to love me. Or maybe it's more that I'm desperate for someone to love."

"Don't say that as if it's a bad thing."

"It is a bad thing to want something so desperately it blinds you to reality."

"No, it isn't. Because you were made to love somebody, Casey. Somebody worthy of you. Somebody you can have children with."

"You don't need a man to have children anymore," she said. "I think it's safer to use a sperm donor. It's more scientific, don't you think?"

He swore under his breath.

"What?"

"Remember I told you when I kissed you that I knew you were never going to be a nun?"

"I remember," she said dreamily.

"Well, you aren't going to make babies like that, either."

"I am so," she said stubbornly. "I've already decided. That's going to be my Christmas present to myself. My gift to myself for the rest of my life. A baby. A child. A family. I'm not waiting for some man to come and give me what I want. I am creating my own life!"

"Is this the major decision Emily told me you were making?"

"Emily told you?"

"Don't do it," he implored her softly. "Casey, raising kids is a tough enough job for two people. Wait it out. Wait for the right guy. The life you always dreamed of is waiting for you. I promise."

"You can't know that. You certainly can't promise me that."

"Yes, I can. Some man is going to see you and *know* what you are. He's going to see that you're funny and brilliant and have a heart of pure gold. And he's going to love and cherish you and protect you, and wake up every morning and look into your eyes and see your amazing hair cascading over his pillow, and he's going to thank God for you. He's going to love having wild-haired children with you."

Suddenly, in all this sharing of secrets, Casey needed to tell him the biggest one of all.

Her defenses were so completely gone it felt as if they had been silly in the first place.

"I want it to be you," she whispered. "I've always wanted it to be you. From the night I met you at Emily and Cole's wedding. I want you to be that man."

He touched her hair with infinite sadness, and with no surprise, as if she had never kept her secrets hidden from him at all. "It can't be me, Casey."

"Why?"

"Aside from the fact you're seeing me in a very heroic light right now, I can't give you what you need."

"Why?"

"Casey, I'm so much like your father, you would run."

CHAPTER FIFTEEN

"YOU ARE NOT!" Casey said. Why had she done that? It felt as if she had peeled open her chest and shown him her very heart. But even so, she felt the need to get at his truth. "You are absolutely nothing like my father."

"I don't mean I'm a womanizer," Turner said. "But I have made choices that pulled my family apart as surely as your dad's way of dealing with life did yours."

It penetrated her exhaustion that Turner was doing what he did so well. Trying to distract her. Maybe even to sting her with his rejection, so that she wouldn't focus on him.

"Tell me," she whispered. "Tell me, Turner, about those choices."

"I already did," he said, with a dismissive shrug. "Those days with you in New York were my last days in your world."

"Then tell me about that other world. The one

you went to. Tell me where you went and what it did to you."

Suddenly, despite all that had happened to her tonight, Casey did not feel weak, but strong. She felt as if she was seeing Turner as clearly as she had ever seen him, despite his efforts to throw up a smoke screen.

And Casey could see he was struggling, at a deep level, that his very soul was in jeopardy. She knew he was the strong, silent type, and she suspected it was the worst prison of all.

She had just told him her deepest longing. Her deepest secret. That she could love him. Now, she needed to know his. And perhaps, if he told her, some wall would come down from around him, and she could crawl over the rubble, and find him inside....

"Turner, let this cabin be our sanctuary. Let it be the place where we can tell each other anything. Unburden it. And then leave it here."

"Go back to sleep, Casey."

"I'm not going to. Not until you tell me."

"Not even if I beg you?" he said wryly.

"Not even then."

"We could reopen the discussion about underwear."

"You know what? You are trying to use distraction, and it is not going to work. You saved me tonight, Turner. And now it's my turn. To save you.

There's something inside you that is eating you alive."

Turner was silent for a long time. And then he sighed, and something in Casey's heart melted, because it was the sigh of a warrior who had found the place, finally, where he could put down his shield.

He was going to trust her, and it felt as if the wall around him had that first all-important crack in it.

"In a way, it's a story like your dad's. Because a tragedy started it. My father died in the 9-11 attacks on the World Trade Center. He was a financial consultant, an ordinary guy, probably a better human being than most, who went to work one morning and got murdered.

"I was in university when it happened. My only goal in life, up until that point, had been to have as much fun as was humanly possible. Someday, though, I assumed I would settle down, have a family and give the same life to my children that he had always given to me.

"But after it happened, I felt like everything he had always stood for was being threatened. I was taken with a rush of patriotic fever, a desire to make a difference, maybe a desire to vindicate my dad.

"Of course, my family did not see it—my becoming part of that rush of young American men who joined the military to make the world right again—as in any way honorable. They saw me leaving when they needed me most, giving my mother one more loss to deal with when she was already at her most fragile. My brothers accused me of leaving because I couldn't stand the pain.

"And it was only a long time later that I could acknowledge how true that was. I couldn't stand it. I couldn't stand all the tears. To this day, I can't stand tears. I couldn't stand wallowing in it. I had to feel like I was doing something about it.

"I pushed to get into an elite antiterrorism unit. I can't talk about what I did, but suffice to say nothing in my rather sheltered and privileged childhood had prepared me for it.

"Even so, I started my career with a great sense of purpose, a sense of taking control in a troubled world. I expected a life of high adventure when I stepped away from everything I knew, and got a life of unfathomable danger and darkness.

"I got a life where mistakes cost lives. Where the people closest to me paid the ultimate price.

"I watched myself change. I became what that kind of work demanded I be. I became a survivor, jaded and cynical. Being emotionally shut down was an asset that was necessary for survival.

"But I'm nothing if not highly adaptable, so I became what I needed to be. And that has meant leaving everything else behind me.

"I was on an extremely delicate, covert assignment when word reached me that my mother had died. It would have jeopardized months of training, and maybe lives, to leave at that moment, so I made a choice.

"My brothers have not forgiven me, and I don't blame them. I'm not the kind of guy who fits into their world anymore. I'm the kind who puts a mission before my own mother. I already told you I'm the kind who ends up in a bag. Better not to let anyone become too attached to me."

"You're protecting them," she whispered. "You think you're protecting them. From you."

He made a harsh sound at the back of his throat. "You can attach an honorable motive to it if you must, but I don't think so."

"How can they not see who you really are?" she asked. "Even Harper can see it."

"That dog nearly killed you. She is missing a few brain cells."

"I can see it," Casey stated, deciding not to hide behind the dog.

"You can, eh?"

"Turner?"

"Hmm?"

"I think I'm falling in love with you." And then she pulled herself in as close to him as she could, and raised her lips to his.

"I just told you all the reasons you can't."

"My heart isn't listening."

He moaned, a low animal sound of pain, deep in

his throat. He took her chin in his hand and gazed into her eyes.

And then he brushed her cheek with his lips.

"No," he said firmly. She got the sense it was as much to himself as to her.

He jumped off the mattress so fast he took the blankets with him. And then bent to awkwardly cover her.

"I came here knowing I had to make a decision," he said. "Do I try to go back to a fork in the road and choose a different path? Could I? Or do I stay on the path that I have chosen already?"

"I don't care which path you take," she said, her voice trembling. "I will support you in either of them."

He snorted. "You don't know the reality of the path I'm on."

"Maybe not," she said firmly, "but I know the reality of you. Turner, couldn't we just give it a chance? Couldn't we just see each other? Couldn't we just see if there's something there? A future for us together?"

It felt as if she had risked everything as she waited for his answer; every ounce of her pride, every bit of who she was was on the line.

For a moment, she saw a struggle behind his eyes, but then it was over.

"Remember when I said you weren't stupid?" he said harshly. "I take it back. You are missing a few brain cells, just like the dog. And I'm not getting any top marks, either. What did I think? That I was at a pajama party, lying here trading secrets? I can tell you are out of danger. I'm going to go."

"Go where?"

"Back to the inn. I'll return with a vehicle and some warm clothes. You should probably go to the hospital."

"I do not need the hospital!"

"Just for observation."

"Please don't do this."

"No," he said, with quiet finality. "Please don't *you* do this. You think you love me because I rescued you. Because you're experiencing that near-miss euphoria.

"I get it all the time. I get it just before I deploy. That heightened sense of awareness. That feeling of being intensely and incredibly alive. The sense that I can see things everyone else has always missed. It's almost like being on drugs.

"You know the first time I felt that way, Casey?"

She shook her head. She had a feeling she really did not want to hear this.

"The first time I ever felt that was with you. Those days in New York. That was the first time I was going to deploy."

She stared at him.

What they had shared that night hadn't been a magical connection between him and her? It had been some kind of intense reaction to heading into danger that had had nothing to do with her?

"You know what else? You know why I rented that presidential suite at the Waldorf? You think it was just to make you feel special? You happened to be in the right place at the right time.

"I'd come into all this money. I had to get rid of it. I had to get rid of that money from my dad's death. Insurance money. Money for the *victims* of 9-11. I hated that money. I hated it as much as I hated the tears. I wasn't going to be anybody's victim."

She felt the shock of it.

And the betrayal.

She could feel her eyes filling with tears.

He looked at her coldly. "Yeah, that's what a woman would get who was stupid enough to fall for a guy like me. A life full of tears. That's why I left without saying goodbye that morning. I knew you'd cry. And I knew it wouldn't change anything.

"You deserve better. You deserve a man who can take your tears and treat them with tenderness.

"You deserve a man who looks at Christmas with something other than dread.

"You deserve a man who can go to sleep with a clean conscience, who is not afraid of his own dreams. I'm not that man.

"There's soup on the stove. It's still warm. You should probably have some."

And then he turned from her and yanked on his clothes.

"Don't you dare leave me here by myself."

"I'll be back within half an hour."

But somehow, she knew he wouldn't be. Without a backward glance he went out the door and was gone.

The dog dragged herself out of the blanket he had wrapped her in, and went and scratched pathetically at the door.

And then Harper did what Casey wanted to do. She began to howl as if her heart was broken.

Turner didn't come back.

It was Rick and Emily and Andrea who came to find her. It was embarrassing being found naked, rolled up in her blanket like a sausage in a pastry wrapper.

But Rick was a complete professional, and her friends were full of nothing but tender concern.

Casey was too distraught to pretend she didn't care. "Where's Turner?"

"He left. There was some kind of urgent message for him from his brother on his cell phone," Emily said.

"But is he coming back? For the vow renewal?" *For me?*

"Cole said he would never let him down," Emily said.

"But?"

She shrugged and watched Casey uneasily. "But I don't know. There was something about him when he came back…"

"What happened here?" Andrea whispered.

Casey thought about that. The trading of secrets, the deep trust.

But in the end, what had happened was the very same thing as before. She had fallen in love.

And he couldn't wait to get away from it!

"Nothing," she told her worried friends. "I fell through the ice. He saved my life. End of story."

What she didn't let on was that if it was the end of the story, she wasn't sure how she was going to go on, let alone not be a wet blanket for the vow renewal.

The house was a flurry of activity. A dozen times a day, Casey wanted to leave.

But Turner was already going to let down his friends. She couldn't let them down, too! So she stuck with it.

She decorated. And delivered cookies. She scrubbed the inn until it shone. She decorated the tree and hung garlands and did paint touch-ups.

And at night, by herself, not able to sleep, she would go down to the lake and put on that old pair of skates.

She taught herself how to skate. She tried. She

fell. She dusted herself off, and she fell again. And got up again.

And somehow, it was the skating that helped her come to terms with it.

Life—and love—were exactly like this. There were moments, if you gave it everything you had, and did not hesitate, when you soared. When you floated joyously through ink-black skies, nearly able to touch the stars.

And then you fell.

But you didn't give up. You brushed yourself off, set your teeth and tried again.

That was what she wanted to teach her child.

A child she suddenly realized she was not ready to have. The greatest gift a mother could give her offspring was to live a whole and healthy existence herself.

When Casey looked at her life, she thought she had played it way too safe. The Gingerbread Girls had been right. She had given her life to a dusty old lab, because there were *rules*. Because it made her life predictable. And to spice it up she had chosen calligraphy? Yoga? Sebastian, for goodness sake?

She needed to skate. And climb mountains. And jump from airplanes.

She needed to love, *fearlessly*.

She had come to the inn searching for something she had searched for her whole life. A Christmas miracle.

Her miracle, it seemed, had come with a crash through the ice, a sudden realization that life could be over in a flash. There was no time to waste on self-pity. Or safety.

Life didn't make any promises. It involved loss and heartbreak.

But, like skating, if you stayed down, if you let the fall cripple you, the joy was gone, too.

She was glad she had laid it all on the line for Turner. She was glad she had risked everything. Because it felt in doing so, she had learned the fall would not kill her.

Not risking at all was what would kill her. In increments, her life getting smaller and smaller as she tried to make it more and more safe and secure.

Casey didn't feel broken by Turner's rejection as she had by Sebastian's. She understood it was about him and not her. She might have risked her heart on Turner, but dammit, she felt as alive as she ever had!

Skating alone, she thought about going through the ice, and the night in the cabin, and she got the gift she had always hoped for.

She knew she was going to be okay. No matter what.

No matter what her mother did. No matter what happened in Emily and Cole's future, or Andrea and Rick's, Casey was going to be okay. No matter what Turner decided to do, she was going to be fine.

Her amazing life had given her the tools she needed to live deeply and fully. To embrace it all, and then to get up and soar on.

And so on Christmas Eve, as Casey put the final touches on the snowmen, she felt loss and joy intermingled, as they often were in the tapestry of life. She adjusted the top hats and ties on the snowmen, and let a few tears fall as she remembered the fun she and Turner had had in the snow.

And then she allowed herself to smile at how adorable the snowmen looked, and to be grateful to have made this contribution to her friend's happiness.

The truth?

Casey had loved her brother. And her father. And her mother. She loved Turner. And even though each of those loves had not been predictable in their paths, each had made her a better person, not a worse one.

Knowing that was her very own Christmas miracle.

And she knew something else. That perhaps she had never loved Sebastian at all. That, in a way even hidden from herself, she had seen him as a means to an end. Perhaps she had seen what she felt for him as safe, because so little of herself had been invested in it.

She had mourned not his loss, but the loss of her own wish for herself: to lead a safe, comfortable, normal life.

And now she saw she had been saved from an unworthy dream. Because love was many things, but "safe" and "comfortable" were not among them.

Real love required people to grow and stretch and become more than they were before, not to stay in a comfortable rut.

"The hairdresser is here," Andrea called, pulling Casey away from her contemplation of the snowmen.

Despite her pleas to straighten her hair, the hairdresser did it in a regal upsweep. When Casey looked at herself in the mirror, it seemed the way her hair was done reflected the great growth she had experienced since her near-death experience on the ice. Her curls had been tamed into the updo, but wayward strands broke free, and the result was breathtaking.

Tears stung her eyes as she looked at herself in the mirror and felt total self-acceptance. Love was breathtaking.

She walked through the inn and on outside. Darkness had fallen and the Gingerbread Inn looked as if it had been restored to all its glory.

It looked like something out of a winter fairy tale. The snowmen were a lighthearted touch at the gate. All the Christmas lights were on. The porch

railings were covered in garlands of real fir boughs.
A huge wreath hung in the doorway. As darkness
fell, Carol and Martin lit the candles in white paper
bags all over the yard. They looked like fairy lights
and the yard looked like something out of a dream.

Not knowing they were being watched, the two
of them paused. Tears stung Casey's eyes for the
second time in just a few minutes when Martin
swept Carol into his arms and kissed her long and
deep.

And then they both turned back and looked at
the inn, and whether they were aware of it or not,
Casey knew what their future held.

Each other, and the Gingerbread Inn.

The inn had never looked so beautiful as guests
began to arrive. Carol and Martin welcomed them
and showed them to their seats, arranged in a half
moon around the front porch. Carol was glowing
with pride and with something else. The joy of a
woman who had said yes to love.

Turner wasn't here.

He wasn't coming.

Somehow, Casey had thought she might have
one last chance.

CHAPTER SIXTEEN

As she and Andrea stood, gazing at the fairyland of wonder they had created, a cab shot up the driveway and Turner hopped out, suit bag over his shoulder.

"Turner," Andrea said to him, hands on her hips. "Turner Kennedy, you have caused me a great deal of stress."

Casey could feel her heart beating in her throat when she saw him. This was what love felt like, then.

Wanting what was best for him, even if it was not what was best for her. But what if what was best for both of them was the very same thing?

Turner's gaze was like flint. "You don't know the meaning of the word *stress,*" he told Andrea.

He glanced at Casey, and the flintiness did not leave his expression.

But she saw the exhaustion around his eyes, the deep weariness.

"You haven't been sleeping again," she noted quietly.

Andrea seemed as if she was going to say something to him, and then stopped, glanced at his face, glanced at Casey beside her, made a sympathetic little clucking noise and flounced into the house, leaving them alone.

Turner brushed by Casey without saying a word. He left her standing on the steps, shaking with so many mixed feelings she felt she might explode. Could love be mixed with so much anger and frustration and confusion?

She went to her room and got ready. The dresses she and Emily and Andrea had chosen were beautiful. Hers and Andreas were navy blue, each with a slightly different cut. With the upswept hairdo and the elegant dress, Casey was not sure she had looked so beautiful at Emily's first wedding. After a final twirl before the mirror, she went downstairs.

She reminded herself, firmly, that this night was about Emily and Cole. Her personal agendas had to be set aside.

A few minutes later, Turner was also back downstairs, looking unfairly amazing in a beautifully cut suit that showed off the tremendous masculine power of his physique.

He looked at her, his gaze taking in everything. She shivered from the hunger she thought she saw there. But, no, now it was gone, if it had ever been there at all. His face was carefully schooled in a calm mask.

"We need to talk," she said to him in an undertone.

The grim line deepened around his mouth. "Yeah, we do. About you interfering in my life. You sent a message to my brothers?"

"You won't have to worry about that happening again."

"You can't unring a bell." But for all the harshness in his tone, for a moment she saw something baffling in his eyes. A woman determined to be dumb might mistake it for regret.

But the flurry of last-minute instructions from Andrea, and their respective duties, drew them apart.

The yard was completely dark now, except for the golden light on the porch, the Christmas lights on the house and the flickering candles, luminescent in the white bags. People were seated in a semicircle around the porch. The wedding party stood inside the door.

Andrea pressed Play on the CD player, and a song by a children's choir came on. Their voices were soaring and joyful, and filled the night. The song was about love being a light to follow through the darkness.

When it was over, Andrea signaled to Casey and Turner. They went out the door together, then parted, moving to either side of the porch. Andrea, and Cole's other best friend, Joe, did the same.

And then Cole stepped out, and waited for Emily.

Emily had decided on a simple ivory frock and a matching cashmere sweater. She was carrying a single bloodred rose as she stepped toward her husband.

A collective sigh went up from all assembled.

There was no mistaking the look of exquisite tenderness Cole gave Emily. There was no mistaking her absolute love for him, as she rose on her tiptoes and brushed her lips against his cheek.

They were both shining from within.

In a simple ceremony that took only ten minutes, Cole and Emily took those sacred and ancient vows. Cole did not have to repeat them after the minister, but said them as though they were written on his heart.

"I, Cole," he said in a voice strong and true, sure and steady, "renew my vow to you, Emily, to love you as my wife, to have and to hold, for better or for worse, for richer or for poorer, in sickness and in health, to love and to cherish, until death do us part."

Then Emily, quiet, strong, said those vows also.

It was as if every bit of hard work they had all done to the inn disappeared, and every single person. It was as if Emily and Cole stood alone, wrapped in their love for each other.

When their lips met, for a moment there was only silence.

And then a cheer went up, as those invited realized they had been part of a miracle, the affirmation of love in a world where it could be so hard to find it, so hard to sustain it, so hard to keep its light from going out.

Wasn't that really what Christmas celebrated, after all? The very thing these two people were re-affirming on this beautiful Christmas Eve?

The way Cole and Emily continued to look at each other—as if each was brand-new to the other—made Casey's throat close.

Turner put his hand on Cole's shoulder. It was a gesture of solidarity, and it made Casey glance at him.

And what she saw made her heart stand still.

For one unguarded moment, as he looked at his friend, the remoteness left his face. And in its place was the deepest yearning that Casey had ever seen.

Turner wanted what his friend had just said such a resounding yes to.

But then he glanced at her, and the look was gone. He took his hand from Cole's shoulder and shoved it deep in his pocket. Turner narrowed his eyes and held hers coolly, daring her to believe what she had just witnessed.

But she did believe it.

It was as if the Christmas miracle she had waited for her entire life had been delivered in that one unguarded second when she'd seen the yearning in a strong man's face.

But the moment was swept away as people left their chairs and surged around Cole and Emily, hugging, crying, congratulating, laughing.

Everyone was invited in. The house was as it was meant to be, at last. Filled to the rafters with people laughing, and loving each other.

"I can't thank you all enough," Emily said, after a while, silencing the mingling crowd with a lift of her hand. "My two best friends, Casey and Andrea, have made this day perfect for me and my other best friend, Cole. And I am humbled that so many of you were willing to spend your Christmas Eve with us.

"There's skating outside, and hot chocolate by the barrel, so I'll see you out there for our first dance in about ten minutes."

Casey joined the crowd who watched from the bank. Emily and Cole had elected not to change their clothes. They looked like pairs skaters waiting to take their turn in a fancy competition.

What followed was poetry. A dark night, white snow, Emily and Cole skating hand in hand. And then he pulled her to him, and she twirled into his arms, and they skated seamlessly, a gold medal performance because of the genuine love that shimmered around them.

It was one more beautiful moment in an evening that had strung together beautiful moments like pearls on a thread.

Casey couldn't help but fantasize that it was she and Turner out there skating, but then jerked herself to reality. He had disappeared as soon as the ceremony was over. But he had arrived by cab, and one hadn't returned to pick him up.

Was he still here?

She pulled herself away from the crowd and went to change out of the beautiful dress and remove the pins from her hair.

She couldn't go out there to the rink, and visit and drink hot chocolate and show off her new skating skills, and pretend everything was all right. She couldn't. She had to find Turner and talk to him now. She wondered if maybe he had slipped away already.

She knocked on the door of his room. At first she was relieved that she could hear him in there, and but then there was sudden silence.

No answer.

She tried the door, and it opened. She took a deep breath and stepped in.

Turner had not changed from his suit, though he had stripped off the jacket, loosened his tie at his throat. He was sitting on the edge of the bed with his head cradled in his hands. When she entered, he shot up off the mattress, his position defensive.

She knew she had caught him at a vulnerable moment. "We need to talk."

He shrugged, all his defenses in place now.

"Being found in that cabin, naked except for a blanket, was one of the most embarrassing moments of my life," Casey said, hoping she had stripped every bit of the hurt and despair of the last few days out of her tone.

"Then you've led way too sheltered a life. I am so angry about you sending a message to my brothers. That situation was none of your business. What on earth made you think you should contact them?"

"I could see you were dying of loneliness."

He drew in his breath sharply. For a moment, he couldn't speak. When he did, much of the anger was gone from his voice.

"You scared the hell out of them. An urgent message from someone they had never heard of? They thought something had happened to me."

"And they contacted you to make sure you were all right?"

"The message was waiting for me when I got back from the cabin."

"It seems to me that would be an indication your relationship with them is not as damaged as you thought. They care about you. It was as good an excuse as any to hightail it out of here, though."

He was squinting at her dangerously. She was sure it was a look he could have used to intimidate the enemy.

But she could not let it work on her. It felt as if her life—and his—depended on that.

"I figured it out," she said softly. "It's not about them. And it's not about me. It's about you. The big, tough soldier. Terrified."

He looked at her warily.

"For a smart woman, I can be kind of dumb sometimes."

"You're preaching to the choir. I saw you nearly die trying to save a dog."

"Hmm," she said. "Dumb about matters of the heart."

His look of wariness increased.

"I meant it when I said I was falling in love with you." How had this happened? She was saying the exact opposite of what she had planned to say if she ever saw him again!

But what could possibly be gained by lies?

She suddenly understood the absolute necessity of standing in her truth, of being who she really was, of not hiding.

"Well, there's the dumb part," he said.

But she looked right past the harshness of the words.

"Remember when you told me you were like my dad? And I said you weren't? You are in this one way.

"I figured out you think you have to protect everyone and everything. You feel it's your highest calling to protect what is yours, don't you? You even said that."

He didn't answer.

"You said, 'I think every man feels that way. As if it is his highest calling to protect what is his.'"

Turner was silent, and so she went on.

"You told me you had come to rely only on yourself. And when that failed you believed in nothing anymore. What happened?"

His lips pressed together in a hard line.

"What happened?" she said again, dangerously.

"The last mission went bad." He choked this out.

"And was it your fault?"

"No. But a good man died. The best. And it was a reminder."

"Of what?"

Turner glanced at the door. He looked as if he was going to put his hands on her shoulders and push by her without answering.

But she leaned on the door, blocking it with her body.

"It was a reminder that when it matters most, a man is powerless. I couldn't save my dad, and I spent all those years trying to change that. Only to arrive in the same place. I couldn't save anything.

"Don't you see what a man who has lost all faith would bring to you?" He asked this desperately.

And she knew, then, that she had won.

That he was breaking wide-open in front of her.

She crossed the distance between them and looked up into his face.

"Poison," he told her, desperately. "I would bring all the ugliness I have seen and been to you. And to my brothers. I'm going back after the holidays. I am going back to what I do."

"What was his name?" she asked softly.

There was a long silence, and when his voice came, it was a whisper.

"Ken. Ken Hamilton. We called him Ham because he was such a practical joker. He had a wife, Casey, he had kids."

"I'm so sorry."

"I didn't protect him."

She let that fall into silence. For a long time, she said nothing. A huge shudder shook him.

"Who protects *you?*" she asked.

"What?"

"You are trying so hard to protect everyone, to save the world. Who protects you? Who saves you?"

He stared at her silently, as if he did not comprehend the question, or was afraid of the answer.

"I do," she said. She held out her hand.

He stared at it for a long time. She did not take his hand, or move hers. She waited. This step had to be his. And then, hesitantly, he put his hand in hers. And she drew him to her, and guided his head to her breast, and felt him give a great sigh against her.

"I do," she said again. "I do."

In the distance, she became aware of people

calling out farewells to one another, the air full of Merry Christmases.

Car doors began to slam, engines to start.

For a while there were the sounds of things being put away downstairs. And then that, too, was gone.

Casey held Turner Kennedy, and was aware she would hold him for as long as it took. She guided him to the bed and he lay down, and then she lay down beside him and stroked his face.

"Not just for tonight," she whispered. "I'm going to wake up beside you tomorrow, and every Christmas after that for as long as we both shall live."

"You need to know who I really am before you say that."

"You think I don't know that?" she said, gently scoffing.

"I come with a lot of baggage," he warned her. "Unusual fears. I'm terrified of tears."

"You're a man that dogs love," she told him tenderly.

"And I have problems sleeping." But for a man who had problems sleeping his voice was growing husky, and he yawned deeply.

"Children love you, too," she said with deep satisfaction.

"I have a job that is hard on the people who love me."

"I'm sure your brothers and I will bond over that. But yes, if you want, we'll take it slowly."

"I think we should go serve dinner with your mother tomorrow night," he said.

"We could put that off for a bit."

"No, we couldn't."

She could feel all the tension draining from him.

"I think I owe you a few days at the Waldorf." His eyes were closed. The steady in-and-out of each breath was coming further apart. "Do you want to run away with me?"

"Yes," she said. "Yes, I do."

"Not for three days. Not this time, Casey. Do you want to run away with me forever?"

"Yes," she said, without a moment's hesitation. "Just be warned. The next time you get down on your knees in front of me?"

"Yeah?"

"It won't be to paint my toes or tighten my skates."

"All right," he said, his voice husky. "I consider myself warned."

And then he slept, and she slept, too. His sleep was dreamless, but a different dream began that night.

It was a dream realized, a dream of being safe. And loved. It was a dream of belonging. And it was a dream of coming home.

It was a dream all the more cherished for the fact that it had once been given up on, seen as unobtainable and dismissed as impossible.

That was what love did—made the cynic a believer, made the fearful brave. Made a man who had lost faith in everything embrace the possibility of miracles.

EPILOGUE

"UNCLE TURNER, THE fireworks are starting in two minutes. Come outside."

"Just a sec."

"No. *Now.*"

Turner dragged his eyes away from the book he was studying, and looked at Tessa. She was eight, as bossy as ever, and the unchallenged queen of a new set of Gingerbread Girls that included his own seven-year-old niece, Hailey.

"Hasn't your dad told you not to go into people's cabins without knocking?"

"The door was open," Tessa said. "And I'm not really *in.*" She waggled a foot at him to demonstrate it was outside the door. Hailey giggled approvingly.

It was the Fourth of July, and the Gingerbread Inn was full. He and Casey had rented one of the new cabins that Martin and Carol had added last year. They were quaint little log buildings facing Barrow's Lake, set back from the main inn. Turner had hoped for a bit of privacy so that he could study for a particularly tough exam.

He had left all the doors and windows open, not just for a pine-scented flow of air on the hot summer evening, but because he liked the background noises. The quiet lap of the lake water against the shore. The evening cries of birds. The snap and pop of a bonfire at the water's edge.

But the sounds were mostly the cries of lots of children. Carol had inherited a passel of grandchildren when she had married Martin. Emily and Cole's daughter was two. Turner's brothers and their wives, and his three nieces and nephews were here.

Next year, at this time, there would be a new baby. He and Casey had chosen not to find out if it was a girl or a boy, but to let life surprise them.

So far, life had surprised them a lot, and maybe especially him.

With its capacity to delight. With its opportunities for love.

That first Christmas he had spent with Casey had been a baptism by fire into the opportunities for love. They had joined his brother David at his brother Mitchell's place to watch the kids open gifts. And then they had gone to help Casey's mother serve dinner to the homeless.

After that was over, Turner had needed a rest. He'd booked a whole week in the presidential suite at the Waldorf.

And they'd done it all again.

Jumped on beds, and worn the white housecoats, and walked to museums and theaters, and eaten wonderful food.

Only this time there was no predeployment intensity in the air. And he'd still felt it: as if every single moment was infused with light.

He'd known the truth then.

Excitement was one kind of high.

And love was another. Quieter. Deeper. More lasting. All those years ago, he'd experienced the dropout punch of them both combined.

Of course, in time, as he wooed Casey in earnest, they had reached that place where he'd had to deploy.

And instead of feeling any of that intensity he usually experienced, he had felt only the sadness of leaving her to deal with a great unknown all on her own. But Casey was the strongest woman he had ever met. And at least he had been working on becoming the man he had always wanted to be.

Because when she cried, he held her and dried her tears tenderly. He saw what an honor it was that a man like him, who had almost turned his back on this most precious of things—love—would be so trusted, so cared about.

It had been easy to make the decision that he had wrestled with for so long. It had been easy to say goodbye to one life, and open the door for a new one.

The easiest thing he had ever done was get down on one knee and ask Casey to walk with him down the winding road that was life.

Were there wounds that he would never quite recover from, no matter what was said about time?

Yes.

But Turner had come to know he had no corner on tragedy. Each of these people who came here, his friends who were closer than friends, his family of choice, had known tragedy. Or defeat of some kind.

Each of them: Cole, Emily, Andrea, Rick, Casey, his brothers, had been tested by life and had known some devastating loss. That was probably the thread that had drawn them together that Christmas when Emily and Cole had renewed their vows.

And yet, woven into the fabric of that loss, were threads of light. Those threads were courage. Compassion. Patience. Forgiveness. Against the fabric of darkness, those threads of light shone as if they were the only important things.

Turner had come to this inn, like those wise men who had followed a star to a stable. He had not been sure what he would find, and he had not even been sure what he was looking for.

What he had found was the miracle he had stopped believing in.

It wasn't a water-into-wine kind of miracle.

It was a quieter kind.

It was the ability to see that the human animal had an amazing resiliency of spirit. People could slog through loss and disillusionment and discouragement to come to this place.

A simple place, where they could pause and stand in the light.

They could come to these moments of pure and joyous life.

The Gingerbread Inn had been restored to being that place where everyone wanted to be with their families.

A place of simplicity in a complex world.

A place of serenity in lives that were full.

A place of utter safety in a world that could be dangerous and unpredictable.

In a few weeks, Turner would be finished with an accelerated program to get his master's degree in business.

He had taken a detour from the life he wanted, but he was not sure that, given the choice, he would change a thing.

Out of all the people here, he suspected he had a deeper sense of how precious all this was.

Of the miracle of peace.

Children's laughter floated in the warm night air. Above it all, he suddenly heard Casey's, which rang out like a kind of truth.

"Are you coming?" Tessa demanded.

He put away the books and stood up and stretched.

At the door, Tessa took one hand and Hailey took the other, and they pulled him eagerly to where a fire burned brightly on the shore of the lake.

In the distance, he could see Martin preparing the fireworks that he would shoot off over the black, still waters.

Turner moved toward the sound of Casey's laughter, with the eagerness of a warrior who had been allowed to lay down his sword, who needed to fight no more.

He headed toward the sound with the heart of a man who had lost his way, and then found it.

As if she knew he was coming, Casey turned and searched the darkness until she saw him.

He headed toward the welcoming light in her eyes with the firm and utterly fearless step of a man who knew his way home.

* * * * *

REQUEST YOUR FREE BOOKS!

2 FREE NOVELS
FROM THE ROMANCE COLLECTION
PLUS 2 FREE GIFTS!

YES! Please send me 2 FREE novels from the Romance Collection and my 2 FREE gifts (gifts are worth about $10). After receiving them, if I don't wish to receive any more books, I can return the shipping statement marked "cancel." If I don't cancel, I will receive 4 brand-new novels every month and be billed just $6.24 per book in the U.S. or $6.74 per book in Canada. That's a savings of at least 22% off the cover price. It's quite a bargain! Shipping and handling is just 50¢ per book in the U.S. and 75¢ per book in Canada.* I understand that accepting the 2 free books and gifts places me under no obligation to buy anything. I can always return a shipment and cancel at any time. Even if I never buy another book, the two free books and gifts are mine to keep forever.

194/394 MDN F4XY

Name	(PLEASE PRINT)
Address	Apt. #
City	State/Prov. Zip/Postal Code

Signature (if under 18, a parent or guardian must sign)

Mail to the Harlequin® Reader Service:
IN U.S.A.: P.O. Box 1867, Buffalo, NY 14240-1867
IN CANADA: P.O. Box 609, Fort Erie, Ontario L2A 5X3

Want to try two free books from another line?
Call 1-800-873-8635 or visit www.ReaderService.com.

* Terms and prices subject to change without notice. Prices do not include applicable taxes. Sales tax applicable in N.Y. Canadian residents will be charged applicable taxes. Offer not valid in Quebec. This offer is limited to one order per household. Not valid for current subscribers to the Romance Collection or the Romance/Suspense Collection. All orders subject to credit approval. Credit or debit balances in a customer's account(s) may be offset by any other outstanding balance owed by or to the customer. Please allow 4 to 6 weeks for delivery. Offer available while quantities last.

Your Privacy—The Harlequin® Reader Service is committed to protecting your privacy. Our Privacy Policy is available online at www.ReaderService.com or upon request from the Harlequin Reader Service.

We make a portion of our mailing list available to reputable third parties that offer products we believe may interest you. If you prefer that we not exchange your name with third parties, or if you wish to clarify or modify your communication preferences, please visit us at www.ReaderService.com/consumerschoice or write to us at Harlequin Reader Service Preference Service, P.O. Box 9062, Buffalo, NY 14269. Include your complete name and address.

"PERHAPS IT'S TIME WE WENT BACK," Jackson said.

He hailed a horse-drawn carriage and helped her aboard. For a few minutes they sat enjoying the clip-clopping rhythm. He took her hand in his.

"Freya," he said softly, "there's something— I don't know when I'll get the chance to— Please understand and don't hate me again."

"Hate you for what?"

"This," he said, taking her into his arms.

At once she knew that she'd wanted this ever since that night. One part of her mind told her she should be cautious and resist him, but everything else in her knew that she would never have forgiven him if he hadn't placed his lips on hers, tenderly but insistently.

Her response was beyond her own control, making her slip her hands up around his neck, then his head, drawing him closer so that her mouth could explore his more thoroughly. He made a soft, sighing sound and increased his fervour.

"Freya?" he whispered.

"Yes— Yes—"

Somewhere at the back of her mind a warning voice tried to say no, but she ignored it. She would be sensible another time, but for now she could only allow her feelings to take

HREXP1213R

over, driving her toward him, ever closer, ever more desirous.

"I've wanted this ever since last time," he murmured.

"But you said—friendship—"

"I know. But I was wrong. I can't help it. It's there between us and I can't make it go away. *Freya*—"

Whatever answer she might have made was silenced in the renewed pressure of his lips, moving fiercely over hers. Helplessly she abandoned all efforts at self-control and gave herself up to the pleasure that was coursing through her.

It was a kiss of discovery for both of them.

Jackson had followed her in the hope of making this very thing happen, yet even he was caught off-guard by sensations and emotions. He'd imagined himself prepared for those feelings, but nothing could have prepared him for what was happening deep in his heart and his body.

Freya felt as though everything was whirling about her. What was happening now was exactly what she had vowed she would never allow. But she seemed to have been transported to another world, one where her determination counted for nothing.

Willing or not, she responded, moving her lips in soft caresses, sending her own message from a part of herself she'd never known before.

It was like becoming a different person with different thoughts and feelings in a different world. And she knew that she must become this new person—or refuse to become her to her own eternal regret. She must make the decision any moment now, but first she would allow herself to relish the joy that possessed her for one more moment—one more—one more…

Don't miss THE FINAL FALCON SAYS I DO,
available January 2014.

HREXP1213R